The Study of the Poisoned Pen

Charles Fort Historical Mysteries

Book 3

T E Scott

Shuna Publishing 2019

'So it's a book we're writing, or it's a procession, or it's a museum, with the Chamber of Horrors rather over-emphasized.'

(Charles Fort, 'The Book of the Damned', 1919)

This book is for every mother that has tried to write with small children in the house. Ladies, I salute you!

The shipping warehouse on the North side of the river had been abandoned at the end of the last century. Now, apart from the figure at the desk, it was inhabited only by pigeons and rats.

The quill scribbled across the page. It pressed so hard that sometimes it pierced the paper and purple ink spilled into the blotter below.

Words could be weapons. Who was it said that the pen was mightier than the sword? Some idiot or another. What really wounded was not the pen but the words themselves. Words like traitor, words like adulterer, words like thief. Words like murderer.

A fat London rat scuttled across the window ledge in front of the desk. The figure held back a shudder. What a dreadful place. But absolutely necessary.

The pen paused. A boat on the river rang its bell and the sound cut through the stillness like a knife. Was there a moment to stop it all? A moment where the inevitable consequences could be stopped? The pendulum of fate could be stopped in its inexorable progress?

No. The head bent low, the arm shot out, the pen began to write again. There was no hope. Only the page and its words that begged to be written. Without that there was nothing.

When the hand began to cramp the writing finally stopped. As so often, the intellectual had to bow to the physical. What a disappointment.

The hunched figure rose from its work and selected a pristine

1

white envelope from the large pile on the table.

After a few moments it wrote the address.

Mr Charles Fort, His Majesty's Government, Horseguards Parade, London.

The writer sat back and put down his pen, finally satisfied.

Chapter 1

One week earlier

"I need your help, Edward."

The woman in front of me was beautiful, rich and frightened. Her hair was piled up on her head in an intricate arrangement that must have taken her maid hours to produce.

I stoked the fire until the flames licked the top of the lintel. "I don't think you should be here."

"I've got nowhere else to go."

I turned around and saw the tears that gathered in her eyes. "Well, Liz, what do you expect me to do?"

She sniffed. "I expect you to behave as an older brother should. I expect your help."

I sighed. "I've always tried to be a good brother to you. But the situation with our father is... difficult."

"So you never come home."

"That's right. And I'm busy here."

Liz looked pointedly around at the papers flung haphazard around the room. Some piles had been there so long that they had become old friends.

"Well, we may be experiencing a slight lull." I sat down in one of the armchairs next to the fire. After a moment's hesitation Liz did the same.

"Are you going to tell me what's the matter?"

Liz bit her lip and stared into the fire.

"I've been sent some letters. Some anonymous letters. Saying some dreadful things. I need you to find out who sent them. I need you to make them stop."

I reached forward and positioned a small log towards the back of the grate.

"Anonymous letters. And what exactly do they say?"

"They are trying to break up my engagement."

"To the Honourable Henry Fashton. I do read the letters you send me."

I refrained from mentioning what I thought about Liz's choice of suiter. I had never met Fashton, but I knew the type well enough. Rich men with too much free time and too little brain. Of course I knew them. I used to be one of them.

"Well, Henry is a darling. Simply a darling. Far too good for me of course."

"Now Liz, I'm sure you're quite the catch."

She waved her hand in acknowledgement of the compliment. "You see the problem is precisely that. You see, it is to do with how wonderful Henry is. I'm positive that these dreadful letters are from some other girl who has her heart set on him. They are dreadful fishwives in London."

I crossed my arms. "Let me see them then."

"See what?"

"King George's nightgown. The letters, Liz! Come on, hand them over."

With a grim expression, Liz reached into her handbag and pulled out an envelope. She held it out to me as if it were an unexploded ordinance.

4

The letter was written in a shaking hand with the most extraordinary purple ink. A sure sign of mental derangement, I thought.

To Lady Elizabeth Fotheringham of Woodholm House. I am writing as your friend. Call off your engagement to Mr Fashton. If you continue it will only cause embarrassment for both parties. I believe you will understand the significance if I say that your appointment at Brown's Hotel with a young gentleman did not go unobserved. The engagement cannot continue. I am your friend. Do not make me your enemy.

"It is unsigned," I said.

"They generally are, I believe," Liz replied. She seemed to have shrunk as I read the letter.

"So, Brown's Hotel."

Liz looked down at her hands. "There was a man before Henry."

"I believe there were several."

"Now Eddie, don't get nasty. I admit, I like a little attention. And why not? It is dreadfully dull in the country. But this man was... something special."

"Who was he?"

"A navy man. I met him in '17. He had just been invalided out. He was sent to the village to convalesce. He had an old maiden aunt that lived there and he slept in her spare room."

"I never met him."

"You were barely home that year. Whenever you were on leave, he was unwell. By the time the war was over he had

5

gone back to his job in Manchester. I never expected to see him again."

"But you did."

Liz sighed. "A few months ago I bumped into him in London. Quite literally, I saw him on the street. We met up a few times. Just as friends."

"You must have known that was risky."

"I have never been afraid of the occasional risk."

I wondered what Liz wasn't telling me.

"What was his name?"

"Does it matter?"

"Come on, Liz…"

"Michael Colton."

"Could he have sent the letters?"

"No. He wouldn't." Liz held up her hand as I began to protest. "And he's in South America. He left last week."

I put another log on the dwindling fire.

"Where are the other letters?"

"I don't have them. I've been burning them."

"Oh Liz," I sighed.

"I didn't want Henry to see them. I only have this one because Henry opened it by mistake."

"Your fiancé read this?"

"Yes."

"How did he react?"

"He was furious. But he remains faithful to me. It is the scandal that worries him. Worries us both. Please, Edward, say you'll help me."

I had never seen my sister like this before. She was usually so calm and composed.

"It's not exactly my area, Liz. I'm meant to investigate paranormal crimes. Not nasty letters."

"I'm desperate. Henry has threatened to call the wedding off if this comes out. I've managed to stop him for now but he's demanding answers. And I'm frightened that there might be more letters to come."

"How will I explain it to my boss?"

"Tell him a ghost sent them! I don't know, I just know that I need your help."

I walked over and gave her a hug. "Of course I'll help. I'm just not sure how yet."

"Oh Edward, thank you so much." Some of the tension left her shoulders and she sat down on my armchair. And you won't tell mother and father, will you?"

"I haven't spoken to them in months, so you don't have to worry about that."

Liz opened her mouth but I put up my hand to stall her.

"No, I don't want to talk about it. Let's concentrate on one problem at a time, shall we?"

Chapter 2

It was a further half hour before I managed to extricate myself from my sister's clutches. After she finally left, I managed to hail a cab in the street to take me to my rather unusual place of work.

When I arrived at the residence of Mr Charles Fort, paranormal researcher and partner of yours truly, I found the door to the building open. In the hallway were no less than four disgruntled neighbours.

"Tell the bloody Yankee to stop that racket!" The corpulent woman with grey hair had her sleeves rolled up as if poised for a fight.

"What racket?" I began to say but my words were drowned out by a sound that blasted the senses. It was somehow high and low, bass and treble, like a screech from a dying creature.

"I'm going to kill him," said a thin man with a yellow grin and an Italian accent.

"Mr Fort is a consultant to His Majesty's Government," I replied with some gravitas. "I suggest that you desist from making threats against his person."

"He's a bloody nuisance," the large woman said. "Tell that to His Majesty."

I slunk past the angry mob and made my way up the stairs to the Forts' apartment. Another blast of sound greeted me when I reached their door. Against my better judgement, I pushed it open. There would have been no point in knocking.

I walked in on an extraordinary sight. Charles Fort was stripped to the waist and dripping with sweat. Across his chest was a

Spanish guitar which he was strumming tunelessly with one hand. The other hand held what appeared to be a French horn up to his lips. There was a bass drum on his back which operated by strings from the elbows. There were cymbals strapped to his knees and bells at his ankles. It was quite the most ridiculous thing I had ever seen.

I around the room looked for Fort's wife Anna. She sat next to the window with what appeared to be cotton wool jammed into her ears.

"Charles is bored," she said simply.

"I am not bored," Fort put down the instruments. I resisted the urge to fling them out of the window. "I am experimenting with the ability to hold multiple dogmas at once. I came across a case recently that epitomized the evil of modern specialization. The event occurred in Servia in 1889. A seismologist recorded an earthquake, but did not mention any falling rocks. An astronomer noted a fall of heavenly rocks, but no earthquake. Rather than embrace an inclusive concept, these scientists demonstrate their wilful ignorance by considering only their own subjective positions. Thus my attempt to embrace multiple musical themes in one body."

"So all this noise is a just a metaphor?" I asked.

Fort frowned for a moment, then bellowed with laughter. "I suppose it is. I borrowed it from a man I met in the Bull and Hind. Come, Edward, help me out of this thing."

It took a surprisingly long time to extricate Fort from his one man band machine, by which time Anna had made tea.

"I am glad you stopped by," Fort said, his large moustache scattered with biscuit crumbs, "I have some papers for you to read on the Super Sargasso Sea."

"Ah," Fort's favourite topic, but not, I had to admit, my own. "And how does this relate to our criminal investigations?"

"Well, as we have had few of those recently, consider it an addition to your general education in the ways of the phenomenologist. Now, we have already spent many months considering the evidence for the events known as weird rains."

"Many," I agreed.

"These rains – along with thunderstones and other strange objects that fall from the sky – must come from somewhere. I have often posited the existence of the Super Sargasso Sea. It is the realm of the lost, the forgotten things that return to earth to haunt those down below."

Even though I had my own scepticism regarding Fort's opinions I must admit I always enjoyed hearing him speak. But today I was a little distracted.

"Liz came to see me," I said when there was a pause in the Charles Fort lecture.

"Your sister?"

"Yes. She has been getting anonymous letters."

Fort raised his eyebrows. "Unpleasant ones?"

"Indeed. She has asked me to investigate them. Find out who sent them."

"Hardly our usual variety of crime."

"I know, but I felt I could not refuse."

Fort came and sat on the armchair opposite me. He looked a little uncomfortable. The topic of my family was one that we did not often broach.

"I'm not sure that an investigation is the best choice. In your sister's case, I would tell her to burn the putrid things and forget about them."

"It is not quite that simple. She is engaged. To a very important man, apparently. Her position is a delicate one."

"I understand your wish to help her, Edward, but you know that an investigation does not always benefit the victim."

"I know. But what else can I do?"

The American cupped his chin and thought for a moment. "Well, perhaps we could examine the case of the letter writer like any other kind of anomalous phenomena. After all, a person who sends anonymous letters could definitely be considered abnormal."

I felt tightness ease in my chest. "Thank you, Fort. It is good of you to help."

The great man waved a hand distractedly. He was already deep in thought.

"The psyche of the anonymous letter writer is a particularly fascinating one. It often speaks to deep mental unease."

"You think we are dealing with a madman?"

"We may be. But madness itself is merely a disarrangement of the mind that science does not yet understand. What is madness, exactly? No one knows. But in this case, we must try to find out."

Chapter 3

"It is just as one might expect," Fort said as he read the letter. "Short and nasty."

We had retired to the public bar on the next street. I hadn't wanted to discuss Liz's problem with Anna in the house. Besides, the mutterings of Fort's angry neighbours were rather distracting.

"What are your first thoughts?"

"We must examine this letter like any anomalous object. Firstly, its composition." He turned the paper over in his hands. "Cheap writing paper. Found in every stationer, I should expect. No help there."

"Sherlock Holmes would have known the author by the scent of the paper or the slant of the handwriting," I said.

"Mr Holmes is a slave to science. And fictional. I am neither." Chastened, I sipped my pint and relapsed into silence

"To continue. What strikes one most about the letter is the colour of the ink. Surely this suggests an unsound mind. It is at least an affront to good taste. But could it be a red herring? Or, a purple one?"

"What do you –" Fort held up a single finger to stall me.

"So we note the purple ink. But we should not let ourselves be blinded by the obvious. We must look beneath, for the buried, the hidden, the damned. The data that the scientist would overlook, or obscure with his own pedagogy like the eclipse hides the light of the sun."

Fort was only on his second pint. I let out a meaningful cough.

"Yes, well, to return to the case in point. I wonder if the ink itself might point to a more important detail. The writing is wild, yes. Look here, the pen has pierced the paper with its ferocity. But the spelling is intact. The argument is coherent. The message is clear: the engagement must be broken. Do you think this sounds like a person writing in a fit of madness?"

"Perhaps not."

"It is possible then that the scientific eye may miss what the unencumbered mind sees. That we are meant to assume madness when the writer of this letter may be entirely sane."

"Then the author may not be a jealous love rival?"

"If we follow this theory, probably not. If I were you, I would look for this Michael Colton. He would have reason to see the engagement called off."

"Liz says no, but I believe you may have a point. I shall track him down. And I'll see if the Honourable Henry Fashton will take a visit too."

Fort smiled. "You are learning, Edward. Yes, the fiancé's innocence in this should not be presumed either. But remember, this is just one solution of the hundreds that might be true. As I have told you before the seeker of truth will never find it. But the dimmest of possibilities, he may himself become Truth."

"Hmmn?" I said, momentarily lost.

"I mean to say that there is another possibility."

"What's that?

"The letter writer may be just as deranged as he or she appears." Fort turned to face me, suddenly serious. "And if that is the case then your sister could be in great danger."

I stared at Fort, at a loss for words.

A boy ran into the lounge, letting the door slam behind him.

"Mr Fort and Mr Moreton?" He called as he peered into the smoky gloom.

"Over here," I said and he hurried over and handed me a telegram.

Wanted at Horseguards STOP Worthing STOP

"I see the British government are still watching the telegram budget," Fort said as I went outside to hail a cab.

"Too early for a brandy?" Robert Worthing had already poured three glasses by the time Fort and I entered the room. It would have been rude to refuse, even though I generally tried not to imbibe spirits before dinner.

The old man was a stalwart of Horseguards. He had been around so long that he had managed just about every department going. Rumour had it that since the war had ended he was coasting towards a lucrative retirement. He must have annoyed someone, however, or he would never have been landed with overseeing us.

"A good friend got the last bottle from a vineyard near Arras. Whole place was destroyed in '17. It took a dozen packets of England's finest cigarettes before the Frenchman would part with it."

Worthing's eyes glittered, daring me to challenge him but I merely smiled and took a small sip. It tasted worse than sailor's rum.

"Excellent," I said, though I was unable to suppress a shudder.

Worthing bellowed a laugh. "Frenchie still had some tricks left, eh? And who could blame him."

"You wanted to see us?" Fort asked while reluctantly setting his glass down on the desk untouched.

"Ah yes. Now, where was that file?" Worthing rooted around in the pile of papers that threatened to spill over the edge of the desk. I thought I caught sight of a cheese sandwich in amongst the mess. At last he pulled out a crumpled piece of paper.

"We have been alerted by the Constabulary to a series of crimes. Mainly petty theft. But the victims are rather interesting." Worthing passed the paper over to Fort to read.

"Ah, very interesting indeed."

I took the paper once Fort proffered it. There was a list of half a dozen names. I didn't recognise any of them.

"Anyone care to explain this to me," I said, mildly irritated.

"You are looking at a list of some of the finest names in modern English literature," Fort said. "If by finest you mean best regarded by the establishment, of course. Personally, I would better trust the judgement of a South American cane toad than a literary critic, but so be it."

I looked again at the piece of paper. Sure enough, now that I knew the link some of the names were somewhat familiar.

"Still," I said slowly, "I don't quite see how this comes under our expertise. Writers aren't exactly paranormal, are they?"

"I don't know about that," Worthing grumbled, "Have you tried reading any of the so-called modern novelists? Give me a Dickens or an Ainsworth any day."

Fort looked a little disgruntled. I remembered that he had tried his own foray into modern literature. It had not gone well.

"My young partner is correct. There is nothing paranormal

about the members of this list."

Worthing lent back in his armchair and shut his eyes. For one extraordinary moment I thought he might actually go to sleep before he eventually spoke.

"Gentlemen, you are members of this department only on sufferance. To put it frankly, you rank somewhere below the shoeshine boy when it comes to departmental importance."

"But, Sir, we have had some successes," I complained.

"Some, yes. One that involved the arrest and disgrace of a member of this department. And another was in Scotland." Worthing shook his head sorrowfully. "It is a busy time for us here. We are still dealing with the fallout from the end of the war, and we may be doing so for the next decade. We are a country of wounded veterans angry with the state, traitors from the war that still lie undiscovered, militant females, and a general population that is still mourning its fathers, brothers and sons. In short, we are drowning in a mess of our own making. So when there is a crime that is brought to my attention and I have no one suitable then I look for the people that are sitting idle. And that is you."

I had never heard Worthing make such a long speech before. He looked rather surprised himself.

"Well, anyway, back to the case in point. A number of members of the modern literary establishment have been in touch with the police to report a serious of petty crimes. Acts of vandalism, theft, and so on. Each was investigated by the constabulary but no perpetrator was found. Finally there was the theft of a manuscript by a Mr O'Hendry. The deputy Prime Minister is apparently a fan of his work." Worthing pulled a disgusted face. "So he insisted we put our best men on the job."

"Right," I said. Somehow, I did not feel like Worthing considered me to be his best man. "So we are to uncover the thief?"

"If you could do that, I would be most obliged. At the least, you will be seen to be doing something. For some reason, Mr Fort and yourself have developed something of the air of celebrity at Westminster. I cannot possibly think why."

I was rather intrigued by the idea of being a celebrity, but Worthing did not elaborate. Instead we were given the list of names and shown to the door.

As we left Worthing's office, I found the unexpected but welcome figure of Miss Victoria MacMillan standing outside. Miss MacMillan lived at my boarding house and worked as a secretary at Horseguards and sometimes featured in my more wishful daydreams.

"Just doing the post round." She held up a sheaf of letters. The movement swept a loose curl from the bun at the back of her head so that it swept down against her neck. She brushed it away irritably.

"I'll walk you back to the typing pool," I said with a look at Fort.

"See you tomorrow, Edward. We can get started on this list then. Good day, Miss MacMillan."

"What list would that be?"

"Something terribly important to national security?"

"Ha." Victoria, like everyone else in the department, was not unaware of how Horseguards regarded Fort and myself. "Have they sent you after the ghost in the tower yet?"

"Not yet," I said. "Would you like to come to the pictures tonight? They're showing Dr Jekyll and Mr Hyde in Regent

17

Street."

"I'm busy. Here, did Worthing really say that about militant women?"

"Victoria, were you listening in?" I tried to sound shocked.

"I could hardly help it with that booming voice of his. I swear, this department is prehistoric. You'd think the suffrage bill had never happened."

She had changed her lipstick, I noticed. The new one was a coral pink that was perfectly applied.

"What about Wednesday?"

"What?"

"The cinema? Wednesday?"

"Still busy, Edward." She turned into the typing pool without a goodbye. I felt that the meeting could have gone better.

Chapter 4

There was only one place to take tea in Bloomsbury when investigating a literary crime and that was in the majestic dining room of the Russell Hotel. From the acres of coloured Italian marble to the gleaming silverware, the room was the ultimate example of pre-war opulence. I pulled my tweeds tight to my shoulders as a defence against the marble coldness. Charles Fort brushed the crumbs of fruit cake from his substantial moustache and leaned back in satisfaction. It was an excellent tea, especially as the British government was picking up the tab.

"You must recover my Intransigent Delphinium." The young man who sat next to Fort was singularly charmless. His hands were never still, constantly fidgeting with the tea things and his tall gaunt figure and curved nose reminded me of a vulture. Like most authors, he was convinced of his own importance, and talked only of himself. It was a tedious meeting, but the man was first on Worthing's list of victims, and therefore first on ours.

"How did you lose it?"

"Lost? I can assure you that the manuscript was not lost. It was stolen!" The author who wrote under the improbable pseudonym 'The London Rake' but whose real name was Stephen O'Hendry stabbed a sugar cube angrily with his spoon, sending it spinning across the table.

"What leads you to believe it was stolen?" Fort was, for once, displaying remarkable patience with the man. Perhaps as a fellow author the American was able to muster more sympathy than I for this interminable bore.

"I kept the novel in a locked drawer in my desk at home. The key I kept under my pillow. On Thursday morning I awoke, reached for the key and found it missing. I ran downstairs and – to my eternal horror – the desk drawer had been wrenched open, and the papers were missing."

I swallowed some lukewarm tea and considered how I had come to this dreary meeting. As Worthing had intimated, our recent forays into criminal detection had been less than brilliant. In the last month we had been sent to investigate a phantom cat in Hyde Park, a spontaneous combustion in Blackfriars (gas explosion) and now an unexplained missing manuscript. We were truly scraping the barrel.

"What I don't understand is how they managed to get the key out from under my pillow."

"Yes, that is a mystery." Fort looked at me and flicked his eyes towards the man's top pocket. There was the clear outline of a hipflask. Perhaps it was not so surprising after all that someone had crept past him while he slept.

"Do you have any inkling who may have wanted to take the manuscript?"

At this O'Hendry grinned, baring yellow uneven teeth. "I can think of a few people who would be happier if Delphinium never made it to the presses. It is sad to say that singular talent always produces envy in others. I have not been immune from the barbs of those determined to belittle my art in an effort to disguise their own inadequacies."

"So you think someone stole the novel out of jealousy?" I tried not to sound too incredulous, but the author looked at me sharply.

"Perhaps. Or perhaps they had heard rumours about the subject matter. You see, my Delphinium is no ordinary novel. It is a work of satire, with my pen pointed at those in our literary establishment that deserve the harshest of critiques. I believe that someone, frightened by the truth of my words, has removed the novel to prevent its publication."

"And you have no copies of the book?"

"I have notes here and there. But no full copy, alas."

"So who do you believe would be most likely to want to prevent publication?" Fort asked.

"I have a list." The man pulled some crumpled pages from his pocket that were covered in spidery handwriting. He looked around before handing it over as if anyone might be interested. I struggled not to roll my eyes as I took the grubby paper from him.

There were seven names, some familiar, some not. I handed it to Fort and he read them aloud, dropping his voice as O'Hendry glared at him.

"Mr Leonard Woolf. Mrs Leonard Woolf. Miss Eliza Darlington. Mr Lytton Strachey. Mr St John Cutler. Mr Francis Simmonds."

I glanced at Fort. Each name on the list, with the exception of the Woolfs, was also on the document that Worthing had given to us. I began to feel that Mr O'Hendry might not be quite as paranoid as he seemed.

"And you consider all of these people suspects?"

"Every one of them would love to see my novel fail. I'd start with Cutler, the cretin that he is. He's your best bet."

"All right," I said. "And we shall need to see the scene of the crime."

"Of course. Come by any time. I work all hours. One never knows when the muse may strike."

"What was your opinion of Mr O'Hendry?" Fort asked when we left the opulence of the Russell Hotel and began the walk home.

"I'm afraid the man is a fool."

"A very great fool. But sometimes the fool can be more illuminating than the genius."

"Is that true in this case?"

Fort thought for a moment. "Possibly not. But there is the absence of a manuscript to account for."

"You're going to tell me about your theory of lost things aren't you?" I said wearily.

Fort's face filled with joy. "My dear Edward, you do listen sometimes! Yes, I was just contemplating that very theory. Whole tribes have been lost from the earth in mysterious circumstances. Why not one manuscript?"

"Indeed." I said, while wondering if O'Hendry might have simply left the thing in the pub.

"We do not know where these objects go. Nor do we know from where anomalous objects appear. Perhaps it is through beings not of this world. Perhaps it is from people who walk among us with extraordinary talents. Perhaps it is some strange realm above us where material things shimmer in and out of existence."

"Perhaps it was a common or garden thief."

"Always the mundane answer, my friend."

"Sorry."

Fort sighed. "I'll visit the library. I must examine the archives for any cases that may illuminate that of Mr O'Hendry's lost book."

He hurried towards the train station. I watched his portly figure retreat, wondering, not for the first time, if there really was a chance any of his theories might prove useful.

With Fort otherwise occupied, I decided it was time to do a little work on our other case, that of Liz's mysterious letter. I stopped off to place a small advertisement with the Times before walking to Scotland Yard.

I had to wait only a few minutes to see Chief Inspector O'Connell. Charles Fort's relationship with the constabulary was somewhat ambivalent, so we were not always welcome. However, after a few false starts, I had in the past enabled the man to arrest a multiple murderer in the last year, so O'Connell still saw himself in my debt. This was good, as I was in need of a favour.

"I'm afraid I'm not here on Ministry business," I said.

O'Connell was London Irish and had thick red whispers that made him look rather comical. I knew, however, that the man was no fool, and he looked unimpressed by my confession.

"Then why are you here, Mr Moreton?"

I looked up at the ceiling for a moment. "I need some information on a Mr Henry Fashton."

O'Connell frowned. "I've heard the name. Something minor in politics, wasn't he?"

"I believe so."

"I don't mind doing you a favour, Mr Moreton, but would you care to tell me what this is about?"

I decided to come clean. "He is engaged to my sister. She recently received a threatening letter telling her to give up the engagement. My partner has suggested the possibility that the letter writer might be in some way connected to Fashton."

"I understand. May I see the letter?"

Liz hadn't actually forbidden me to show the police, so I decided it was worth the risk. I passed it over to O'Connell.

As soon as he saw the letter the detective's face changed to one of acute interest.

"What is it?" I asked.

Instead of answering, O'Connell walked over to a filing cabinet behind him. After a few moments rifling through a drawer he handed me a piece of paper.

My lips parted in surprise. It was the twin to the letter that Liz had received. The same scrawled handwriting, the same dreadful purple ink. Only the content was different.

To Bishop Gaskell. I am writing as your friend. I suggest you do not contest the position of Archbishop next month. Otherwise information about a certain expedition in the Orient will be made public. You would do well to remember events at the Silver Tree Inn. Should you pull out of the election, no further action will be taken. I am your friend. Do not make me your enemy.

"This letter was sent to a friend of mine. Gaskell might be a Bishop, but he's an old army chaplain and he's no soft case. Came around straight away with the letter, and said that whoever wrote it could do their worst."

"It is the same man!" I said.

"Or woman. Most poison pen writers seem to be female I'm afraid."

"Did the Bishop say what the expedition was that the letter mentions?"

"He couldn't stop talking about it. It was a missionary expedition to the Far East. They had a pretty dreadful time of it. The Inn was somewhere they stopped when half the expedition came down with malaria. Eight of them went into the inn, and only three came out, the Bishop and two others."

"And the letter is suggesting that something untoward went on?"

"That was what so incensed poor old Gaskell. Most of the men that died were his friends. One was even his brother-in-law. So he stormed over here and asked me to investigate."

"What have you found out so far?"

"Not much, I'm afraid. I'm tracking down the other survivors from the expedition. It just might be possible that one of them sees the opportunity for blackmail."

"But the letter writer didn't ask for money."

"Yes, that is curious. But this may only be the first letter of many."

"Liz said she received several letters, but she burnt the rest."

"Ah, that is a shame."

I straightened my waistcoat. "Do you mind if I speak to Gaskell?"

"I'll send him a telegram and let him know you're coming. He's a man of faith, he won't turn you away, especially as you both want the same thing. And I'll look into Fashton for you."

"I owe you."

"Not for the first time."

Chapter 5

I recounted my meeting with O'Connell to Fort at breakfast the next day. The American was out of favour with Anna – something to do with him commandeering their wardrobe to store his latest collection of index cards – so I had offered to buy breakfast in a nearby café.

"The Chief is a good man," Fort said, "if a little unimaginative. Still, I expect if there is anything to be found out about your sister's fiancé, he will do the job admirably."

I grunted assent, my mouth full of bread and dripping.

"I wonder, however, why you didn't mention the other party, Mr Michael Folton, was it?"

"Michael Colton. Nothing gets past you, does it?" I said with a smile. "I have not forgotten him. In fact, I have a plan to discover exactly who the man is. I hope to implement it this afternoon."

Fort shrugged. "Well, that leaves us this morning to do some work on the missing manuscript."

"Come along then," I said, wiping the grease from my chin with a napkin. "Let's visit Mr O'Hendry's garret."

O'Hendry's house was rather grander than I had expected. Just on the edge of Bloomsbury and Holburn it was an old Georgian building where he resided in the two upper floors.

The street was broad and tree-lined and we could hear small birds singing up above. I watched as the milkman left two sparkling bottles on the doorstep then hurried off on his rounds.

"Not exactly the home of a starving author," I remarked.

"Yeah, there's money here somewhere."

We walked up the steps to O'Hendry's front door. Here there were signs that a creative mind lived therein. One of the panels on the door was cracked but had been taped over instead of repaired. A huge Doulton vase that might have once come from a country estate was now chipped and cracked with a dying aspidistra that poked out of the top.

I pressed the bell but nothing happened. "Mr O'Hendry?" I shouted but there was no answer.

"Edward, look here," Fort pointed to the inner door which was slightly ajar. "Perhaps we should see if he's all right."

I pushed open the door and walked into O'Hendry's residence. The walls had once been white but were now a dirty grey colour. An Axminster carpet lined the hallway but it was threadbare and stained. Each piece of furniture was of good quality but badly misused. Correspondence had been piled on a side table and overflowed onto the carpet.

"Look here," Fort said. Out of place among the tired Victorian furnishings were a collection of paintings hung on the walls.

They were what one might call abstract art. Blocks of colour and shapes that sat stark on the white canvas. I was about to ask Fort what he thought of them when we heard a cry from upstairs.

I raced ahead to the top of the stairs. There were several rooms off a central hallway. I listened for a moment then burst into the one on the right.

A fug of smoke and stale beer assaulted my senses.

"Damn it, Moreton, what are you doing in my room?" O'Hendry lay on the bed, fully clothed but clearly just awaking from slumber. He was surrounded by a mess of empty bottles and ashtrays. The sense of decay that had permeated the downstairs of the house had taken hold in this room and it was not letting go.

"I'm sorry, sir," I said while trying to ensure that I didn't step in anything sticky, "we heard a cry and thought you might be in trouble."

"We? Is the American chap with you?"

Fort came in behind me. "We were concerned about your welfare. We heard a shout…"

"I dropped my glasses. Can't see a damned thing without them." O'Hendry hunted in the bed until he found the spectacles with a grunt of triumph.

"We came to talk to you about your missing book."

O'Hendry looked startled when I spoke, as if he had already forgotten we were there.

"I've been trying to piece together Delphinium from my notes. It is a thankless task. Like rebuilding a shattered vase. The cracks will always show."

He looked so pathetic that I felt I had to offer some reassurance. "We will do our best to get your manuscript back for you."

O'Hendry merely grumbled something inaudible.

"Would it be all right for us to take a look around your study?" Fort asked.

"Sure. If you think it might help."

O'Hendry lay back down on the bed, clearly not about to show us around. Fort and I left him to it.

The study was a surprise. Unlike the rest of the house it was almost orderly.   There was a large walnut desk with a comfortable chair and a large picture window that backed on to an overgrown garden.

"So, Mr O'Hendry is only messy when it suits him," I said, flicking through a pile of papers on the desk.

"Perhaps he is only the scatter-brained artist when he wants to be." Fort said. "But is it deception or self-deception?"

"I don't follow."

"Well, is it for the benefit of others or for himself that he chooses to present such an image?" Fort picked up a gilded paperweight. "We must find out where his money comes from."

"It is top of my list."

"What about this," Fort said drawing my attention to something above the desk. Pinned to a wall was a faded photograph. It was a group of men and women stood in front of O'Hendry's house. I recognised O'Hendry's hawk like face immediately."

"That's the Woolfs," Fort said, "and some of the others look familiar."

O'Hendry entered the room rubbing his eyes. "See, I told you it was gone."

I blinked. "We never suggested it wasn't."

"Right."

I pointed at the picture on the wall. "When was this taken?"

O'Hendry managed a small smile. "Just after Hogarth Press published my first collection of poems. You know it? 'A London

Rake Gazes into the Mirror'?

Fort and I murmured awkwardly.

"Well, it was highly regarded." O'Hendry looked a little wounded, but carried on. "Of course, I have matured considerably as a writer since then. And 'Intransigent Delphinium' would have been the pinnacle of my life." He turned away, seemingly overcome.

"Who else is in the photograph?"

"Ah, well, here are your prime suspects!" O'Hendry jabbed at the photograph with a grubby finger. "Yours truly, young and naïve on the left. The tiresome Woolfs next to me. Then the venomous Strachey and penny-pinching Cutler. Next the sharp little Miss Darlington. Simmonds is on the end – that was before he got so fat."

"Can we take this?"

"Sure." O'Hendry ripped it off the wall and handed it to me. I placed it in my briefcase.

"And this was where the manuscript was teleported from?" Fort indicated the empty desk drawer.

"Tele… what?" asked O'Hendry.

"Teleported. Transported from one place to another by undiscovered means."

"Ah, yes. Good word that. Maybe I'll use it in my next novel. Yes, the manuscript was stolen from this desk. Nothing else was taken."

"Then it seems that your novel was the target."

"Exactly!" O'Hendry was growing wild again. "It is nothing less than a case of sabotage. When I find out who took it, I will tear them limb from limb." At that moment he truly looked like he might do it.

"Leave it to us, Mr O'Hendry, we will see that justice is served." I said, more confidently than I felt.

"This is a wild goose chase, Fort. The manuscript is probably under his pillow." We had managed to extricate ourselves from O'Hendry's apartments, but I still felt grubby as we made our way back to Horseguards.

"Perhaps. Perhaps not. There are mysteries around Mr O'Hendry."

"He seems to be two different people," I said. "The messy creative genius and the organised man that kept the study so well ordered."

"Exactly. I suspect that there lies the answer to our puzzle."

"What of the other suspects?"

"They are all on Worthing's list of authors who have been targeted by unknown criminals. We should investigate them all to see whether they may be victims or perpetrators. Or both," Fort added.

"Indeed."

A loud roar behind us announced that a large motorcar was barrelling along the street. I turned to watch as a new-minted Crossley purred up the street. With wire wheels and a high lift camshaft it was a vast improvement on the wartime model.

"Edward!" Fort stood beside me a look of exasperation on his face.

"Sorry."

"You and those metal beasts." The American shook his head

sadly. "Shall we meet tomorrow to discuss the case of the missing manuscript?"

"Tomorrow is Saturday. I'm afraid I have a prior engagement."

I could tell Fort wanted to ask what that was, but for once he kept silent. I walked back to my flat, the hum of the Crossley still reverberating in my ears.

Chapter 6

The aluminium chassis felt warm to the touch as I ran my fingers along the clean lines of my Rolls Royce Silver Ghost. It was the perfect day for a race. The sky was clear and it was warm but not too hot. I felt my heart begin to pulse with excitement.

"How's it going, rookie?" Chad Baker was a real American racing legend. Rumour had it he had been poached by the British Automobile Racing Club from Indianapolis at the end of the war. I had pulled in a few favours to convince him to let me race the Ghost alongside the professionals.

"It's my third race," I complained.

"Ah, you'll have to do more than a dozen before I stop calling you rookie. If you last that long." I wasn't sure if that was a joke or a warning. Injuries and fatalities were not uncommon.

I looked up at the curved road of Brooklands and my breath caught. It defied logic that the cars could race round it without tumbling off.

"Well, Lord Fauntleroy, I wish you all the best for today."

"I'm still not happy about the name."

Baker laughed, holding onto his large belly as if it might wobble off. "Now, now, everyone's gotta have a name. It could be worse."

"Is the Sailor racing today?" I asked.

"Yeah rookie, he's just filling up." The man pointed to an old aircraft hangar behind us. I dropped my gloves onto the seat of the Ghost and walked inside.

The garage was full of smoke and grease and men in overalls working at a frenetic pace.

It took me a few moments to spot Admiral Windmore, known by the motoring fanatics as The Sailor. He was sitting in his beloved Austin coupe with mechanics scurrying about the bonnet like a swarm of servile bees.

"Excuse me, may I have a moment?" The Sailor looked at me for a second, perhaps wondering if I were a journalist or someone else determined to interrupt his routine. He spotted the goggles around my neck and grinned.

"You're the chap with the Silver Ghost. Beautiful creature."

"She is indeed," I agreed.

"I can give you a minute while the boys finish her off." He walked me over to a bench that was unoccupied and offered me a cigarette. Close up, the Sailor was older than I had thought, with grey hair at his temples. The way he carried himself spoke of a self-assurance that was ageless: he was still an imposing figure.

"I'm sorry to interrupt your preparations, but I need some help with something I'm working on."

"You're with the Ministry, aren't you?"

"That's right. And I'm looking for information."

"We tend to leave that sort of thing behind us at the track," the man said sternly.

"I know. But I didn't want to take the chance that if I made an appointment you wouldn't see me. You are rather busy after all."

Windmore snorted. He knew that I would know, as would everyone aware of his real name, that he was just about as high up in the Admiralty as one could get without being sent off to retirement in the Lords.

"I need to ask about a man you might have heard of. A navy man, Michael Colton."

"Colton. Invalided out in '16?"

"That sounds like him."

"Now why would a man like you be interested in Mickey Colton?"

I shifted my weight between my feet. "It's rather delicate."

A whistle blew somewhere up ahead. The Sailor pulled down his goggles. "Tell you what, you show me some fire out on the track and I'll tell you about young Mickey Colton. I'll even let you buy me a drink."

"Look out, that Austin's coming up on your left," Jimmy McMill shouted into my ear. Even with him yelling I could barely hear him above the noise of the engine. I changed gear and banked left a little to squeeze the other car out.

"Good show!" My co-driver was an old army friend. Jimmy had been a mechanic with the Service Corps. In peacetime he had scrounged a bit of money together and started his own garage. He had done pretty well for a spanner monkey.

I let out a whoop of excitement. Truth be told I wasn't even pushing the Ghost. This was strictly an amateur race, with no classifications so there were old wartime motors chugging along beside the latest Rolls and Bugattis. I even took the chance to wave at a few families who had come out to watch.

"That's the Sailor up ahead. Think we can catch him?"

I settled down lower in my seat. "I'll be damned if we can't!" I opened up the throttle and the Ghost ate up the road. We were on one of the shorter ends of the oval so I had to work the wheel harder the faster we went. Once we opened up onto the straight, I just let her drift up the bank. It was as if the Ghost was flying. At this speed I could feel every bump and ridge in the track, the vibrations rumbling up my spine.

"You've got him," Jimmy shouted in elation as I put my foot down and cruised up behind the Sailor. I checked my mirrors then flicked the car out from the Austin's slipstream and down the steep curve of the banking.

The Silver Ghost moved past with a roar of triumph. I risked a glance to my right and saw The Sailor give me a brief salute. Two laps later and I saw the chequered flag.

My official position was seventh, but I felt like the winner. I drove the Ghost over to the garage where the eager mechanics began rubbing her down and checking for injuries. McMill bounded out of the car to speak to his friends in overalls but I just sat for a moment enjoying the pounding of my heart in my chest.

"It's addictive you know." I turned to see the Sailor clap his hand on my shoulder. "Watch out or you'll become a slave to the track like the rest of us."

I patted the steering wheel. "I think I may be there already."

"Well, come on then, I owe you a beer."

The little rural pub just down the road from Brooklands was overrun by men in overalls and helmets, like some strange remnant of the war. Except here the atmosphere was rather more jolly.

"What do you want with Mickey Colton?" The Sailor asked,

skipping any pretence at small talk.

"He has come to light in a rather sensitive investigation that I am undertaking."

Windmore took a long drink. "Something to do with a woman?"

"My sister," I admitted.

Windmore raised his eyebrows. "How deep is she in with Colton?"

"I'm not sure." I explained to Windmore about the meetings, Liz's engagement and the anonymous letters.

"Not Colton's style," Windmore said immediately. "He's not exactly a literary type. More actions than words, if you know what I mean."

"So you don't think he would resort to blackmail?"

"I'd believe anything of Mickey Colton, but he'd need someone else to hold the pen if he was planning to write to anyone. Could barely sign his own name that one. Clever enough mind you, in a self-interested sort of way."

"What's his background?"

"He was a good sailor. When he wasn't plotting or scheming. But he always had a cunning way about him. One of those lads that always had better kit than everyone else, that everyone owed favours... that sort of thing. Nothing really bad, maybe skimmed a bit off the top, but no worse than anyone else. Mickey's real problem was women. I was his CO back in '14, just when things were starting to heat up. And the number of times he'd be sent in for messing about with another man's wife. Screwed up his promotion prospects, of course."

"And he was angry about that?" I said, reading Windmore's expression.

"Yes. He got very bitter very quickly. Nothing was his fault, the system was against him, blah blah blah. Not the sort of attitude you want from someone you're stuck at sea with for months on end. It was a relief when he was sent home in '16."

"He was injured?"

"A cordite charge at the Battle of Jutland. Took some shrapnel to his chest. Damned lucky to be alive. Funny the ones that survive." The Sailor was lost in thought for a moment and I cleared my throat.

"Ah, where was I? Yes, Colton. Well, as I said, no one was sorry when he was declared unfit to come back. Some people are just born trouble."

"Did you see him after the war?"

"Once or twice." The Sailor raised his hat to a friend at the bar. "He asked me for a reference in '16."

"You gave it to him?"

The Sailor looked a little uncomfortable. "As I said, he was a good soldier. He took a job with Mainyards, the housebuilders. Think he might have been a foreman. And the last time I saw him, well, that would be last week."

I looked at him sharply. "Last week?"

"He came to see me at work. I have a small office just off Fleet for my consultancy. I was surprised he even knew where it was."

"What did he want?" I prompted.

"He wanted money." The Sailor now looked deeply uneasy. "He asked for a loan. Said he had a new venture, looking for investment, that sort of things. Of course I sent him off with a flea in his ear."

"Colton needed money, then."

"Look, I wouldn't normally say anything, especially about one of my lads. Even a bad egg like Colton. But if your sister's involved in this…"

"I appreciate it."

Windmore sat back in his chair, glad that the conversation was over.

"Will I see you at the track again?"

"Oh, yes. I'm certain of it," I replied.

Chapter 7

"Come in and shut the blasted door, or I'll set the hounds of hell on you."

Bishop Gaskell was not what one might expect from a man of the cloth. I hurried inside his home and closed the door firmly behind me.

"It's Edward Moreton, Sir."

"Moreton? Never heard of you." The voice came from a figure that was hunched over a basket of logs. I moved a little closer.

"Chief Inspector O'Connell sent me."

"Did he now?" the Bishop said and he walked into view. Gaskell was broad shouldered with a deep tan from working outdoors and his liturgical collar hung loose around his neck.

"Are you staring at me boy?"

"Well… I must admit you are a bit of a surprise."

"Did you expect me to keep bees? To study fossils, perhaps?" The anger had been replaced by a more sardonic humour.

"Something of the sort."

"Well, you may find the clergy are not quite the soft creatures we once were. A chaplaincy in the trenches will do that for you."

"I see. And was it that sense of adventure that sent you to the East?"

The Bishop looked at me sharply. "You've read the letter?"

"O'Connell showed it to me. You see, I have a rather personal interest in it. This was sent to my sister." I pulled Liz's letter from my pocket and passed it to Gaskell.

"To send such words to a lady…" Gaskell shook his head. "I thought it was bad enough they would try to intimidate a man of the cloth. Come into the drawing room. I'll have my cook make us some tea."

The tea was dark and strong and the Bishop gulped it down with obvious pleasure.

"Been out in the garden all morning. Good for the soul. Do you get outside much?"

"I live on the third floor."

"Pity. No better way to feel the hand of the Almighty than to grub about in the soil."

Godliness being a little out of my conversational range, I turned the conversation back to the letters.

"You have only received the one?" I asked.

"So far. I was more surprised than anything else when I read it," the Bishop explained. "I hadn't even thought about that sorry time for years. And then when the words sunk in… well, I was really very angry."

"Can you tell me about the expedition?"

Bishop Gaskell rubbed a hand over his face and for the first time he looked his age.

"It was 1909. I had just turned thirty-five and I had been given the promise of a permanent parish in Sussex. I had six months before I could take up residence and a friend of mine offered me the chance to go on an expedition to the Himalayas. I told the diocese that it was a chance to do some missionary work, but really it was an opportunity to see a little of the world. It may surprise you, but even Bishops get bored sometimes."

I smiled. Nothing about Gaskell would surprise me.

"O'Connell said he was trying to track down the other people on the expedition," I said.

The Bishop snorted. "He'll be lucky. Half of them died in that Godforsaken place. Some have died since. There's hardly any of us left."

"Could you tell me exactly who was on the trip?"

Gaskell sighed. "Five of us set out from London. Myself and my sister's husband, Johnny Brown, poor soul. And young Faifley, he was only twenty-three. Then there were two cousins, Jim and Frank Rogers, they were mountaineers. They were the experts, I suppose, although they were just lads like the rest of us. And Adam Walker. He was the one that organised the whole trip. Well, he was the last one to die, after the two young boys. I think it was his heart that broke. He blamed himself you see."

"I'm sorry to bring it all back for you."

The Bishop gave a wry smile. "I sometimes wonder why it is still so painful to contemplate. What were a few lives compared the millions dead in the war? But, of course, we never knew the war was coming. If we had, perhaps we would not have gone looking for adventure. We would have plenty of it soon enough."

"How did the men die?"

"A particularly nasty strain of yellow fever. We had all had malaria the month before, and I suppose our bodies were already weakened. Johnny and Faifley died in their beds before we could even get a doctor out. Adam Walker went a few days later. The two Rogers boys and I pulled through somehow."

"So are they still alive?"

"Jim lived long enough to get blown to pieces at the Somme," the Bishop said in a matter of fact tone. "Frank never went to war, I think maybe our adventure put a stop to that too, he lost his hearing you see. Think he's in a convalescent home in Blackpool. So not many suspects for your letter writer I'm afraid."

"Could it be some relative or friend of one of the men who died?"

"It could, I suppose, but there would be no way to know whom. Faifley was a bachelor, but he may have had some family somewhere. Poor Johnny was married to my sister, of course. She died a widow in '12. I have no idea about the Rogers' family, but then they came home. Adam Walker, now. He was engaged I think," the Bishop frowned. "But I can't remember the young lady's name."

"Well, it's a start."

The Bishop looked tired so I began to get ready to leave.

"What puzzles me," I said slowly, "is how the same letter writer alighted on yourself and my sister for his or her victims."

"That is true. I can't see a connection myself. Could it be mere coincidence?"

"A good friend of mine always says there are no mere coincidences. There must be some connection between you and my sister."

"Well, I'm afraid you'll have to work that one out for yourself." A huge black Labrador padded through and pressed his nose up against the Bishop's leg. "You'd best be off. Mutt here wants his lunch. The Lord's work is never done."

44

"Authors are a delicate bunch," Fort said when we met in the office on Monday morning. "I have tried most of the weekend to arrange meetings with our Bloomsbury set and have met with abject failure."

"But you are an author yourself," I said.

"Ha! One novel and two... well, rather stranger books would not deign to place me in the region of these demigods." Fort said with a scowl. "I may as well have never put pen to paper as far as they are concerned."

I sensed that I was probing at an open wound. "Let me have a try." I pulled over a block of writing paper and began to write to those on our list.

"You think they will want to see you?"

"Not me. But they may open their homes to a dashing young Lord."

Fort snorted. "These are not the type of people to be impressed by a title."

"You would be surprised. Often it is the most socialist of men who are fascinated by the trappings of aristocracy. And, of course, they want to see what a dreadful, decadent dilettante I may be. There is nothing so warming as having one's worst suspicions confirmed."

"You may be right there. Well, have Lord Fotheringham etc etc write to them. Worth a shot."

I did as much, making sure my handwriting was particularly effusive.

"Good," Fort nodded in satisfaction when I showed him the letters. "Now that you have finished you can call me a cab to the British Library. My hip has been acting up and I have no intention of sitting on one of those dreadful trams."

"Fine," I said. "I have some research of my own to do."

"What are you reading, Fort?" The library was cold and airless. Fort may have regarded it as his second home, but I always found it rather dull.

"An account of the life of Lord Byron."

"Now, him I have heard of," I said with a smile.

"I'm investigating the creative mind. Did you know that Byron once said: 'We of the craft are all crazy. Some are affected by gaiety, others by melancholy, but all are more or less touched.'"

I shifted awkwardly in my seat. "Do you believe that is true?"

"What, I, such a well-rounded, stable individual?" I met Fort's eye and we both chuckled. "There may be some truth in it. But is it the writing that drives you mad or the madness that drives the writing? Who's to tell."

"O'Hendry certainly seems the touched creative type."

"Ah, but does he?" Fort leaned forward. "Our Mr O'Hendry is a mess of contradictions. The money in the house doesn't match with how he keeps it. The mess of the bedroom and the orderliness of the study? And even the most paranoid of authors does not sleep with the key to their manuscript under his pillow. No, there is more to the puzzle of O'Hendry, we just cannot see it yet."

Fort closed the Byron book and placed it carefully on the green felt table top. "You have heard me talk about wild talents."

"Many times. Your theory that some people have exceptional abilities."

"Quite. Well, what is creativity if not a wild talent? The ability to excel at artistry, could that not be considered something above the usual human experience?"

"Perhaps."

"And if authors have one wild talent who is to say that they do not have others?"

As usual I struggled to follow Fort's train of thought.

"So you think that our thief…"

"Could be a fellow author with a talent for impossible theft, or the telepathic removal of objects. Or something else entirely."

"And that is the focus of your investigations."

"For the moment. Although I have not ruled out another cause."

"You never do." I leaned back in my chair and folded my arms.

"How is your investigation into the anonymous letter coming on?"

"I am firmly in the research stage." I filled Fort in about my meeting with Gaskell.

"It strikes me that in most crimes we consider the criminal." Fort said, dropping his voice so as not to raise the ire of the librarians. "What he did and why he did it, and how. But here we may consider not the criminal but the victim. For if the letter writer is attacking some incident in the lives of his or her victim, then we may discover their identity through that action."

I thought this through in my head. "I agree," I said slowly. "That is why I am trying to discover more about Gaskell's expedition. The identity to the poison pen must be contained in that history."

47

"And you should do the same for your sister. If you take these two facts and draw the connection between them you will find your criminal."

A librarian appeared silently at my shoulder and passed me a newspaper.

"What's that?" Fort asked as I flicked through the pages.

"I'm looking for something... ah, here it is. It's the account of Gaskell's expedition."

"When the men died?"

"Exactly. It was in South West China on the border with Tibet."

"Does the article support what Gaskell told you?"

I skimmed the entry. "It seems to. Hang on, here's something new. 'Also present at that ill-fated inn were a Spanish couple, Senor Felicidad and his wife who sadly succumbed to the same illness.' I never asked Gaskell if anyone else at the Inn died, but he might have mentioned them."

"Make a note," Fort said, pushing one of his little cards over to me. "Anything unexplained is always of worth."

I left the library and returned to my rooms at the boarding house with several more notes but no sense that I was getting anywhere. I sneaked past Mrs Davenport's door lest she come out and badger me for missing dinner, only to bump into Victoria on the stairs.

"I've been looking out for you," she said.

"Have you," I replied, rather pleased.

She held out a piece of paper. "A very smart policeman stopped by. He left you a note."

The note was from O'Connell and I read it with increasing interest. A third victim of the anonymous letter writer had just contacted the police. And I was to have the first go at interviewing her.

Chapter 8

The house smelt of sour lilacs. The offending flowers had been placed in a jug on the hall table and almost managed to mask a pervasive scent of cat. A small, white-haired maid let me in with a curtsy that made her knees crack.

"I'm here to see your Mistress."

"Mr Moreton? She's expecting you. She even put her good teeth in." The maid gave me a warm smile then took me upstairs to the old woman's room.

Mrs Marylebone was confined to her bed but she had contrived to make it a centre of activity. A collection of occasional tables and armchairs flanked the bed, each festooned with cushions, portraits and a haberdashery's worth of Doulton.

"Mr Moreton, please, take a seat."

I perched on the edge of an armchair that was mainly occupied by embroidered pillows of varying shapes and sizes.

"This is Annie. She's been my maid for fifty years. Waiting for me to die for about thirty of them."

Annie the maid gave a little chuckle as she reached up and fluffed the pillows on the high bed.

"Now, don't you mind any of her nonsense, Mr Moreton. She's a sweetie really." The maid shuffled out of the room.

"I am not," Mrs Marylebone said without rancour.

"Are you keeping well?"

"Listen here, Sonny, I'm too old for small talk. Shall we get to the point?"

I took a breath. "I am told you have received some threatening letters."

The old woman squinted at me. "Who are you again?"

"Mr Moreton. From the government, Mrs Marylebone. I was sent to examine your complaint about some letters?"

"That's right." Her dark eyes twinkled and I was pretty sure she was playing the old lady card with me. "Yes, the letters. Nasty, rotten lies the lot of them."

"May I see them?"

Mrs Marylebone rose from her bed with the aid of a thick birch cane. It was a carefully planned operation and I was poised ready to catch her. But the woman was stronger than she looked. She shuffled over to a large roll top desk and began to rifle through the drawers. Just as I was beginning to grow restless, she pulled out an envelope with a grunt of triumph.

"Here they are. When the first two came, I ignored them. But Annie was here when the third arrived and she said to me, Mistress, you shouldn't be putting up with this sort of thing."

She handed me the letter.

To Mrs Marylebone of Highfell. I am writing as your friend. Some information has been given to me regarding the death of a Mr Reginald Platt in Cornwall in 1892. I know this will be of interest to you. I would gladly return this information for a small fee of one hundred pounds to cover my expenses. I am your friend. Do not make me your enemy.

I took out the letter Liz had received. They were practically identical, even down to the dreadful purple ink.

51

"Is that another one?" Age clearly hadn't dulled Mrs Marylebone's eyesight.

"Yes. I'm afraid you are not the only victim."

"I'm sorry to hear it. I am made of strong stuff. A weaker mind might be harmed by this sort of thing."

"I'm sorry Mrs Marylebone, but I must ask. The man mentioned in the letter?"

"Reg Platt? Yes, I knew him. He was a friend of my husband. He drowned in the sea off Cornwall. It was terribly sad, but there was nothing untoward in it."

"Did Platt have any family?"

"None. He was an orphan, the poor thing."

"I see. And what do you think the information that the letter writer mentions might be?"

Mrs Marylebone sniffed. "Some silly rumour or another. It cannot be anything more."

"Were there rumours at the time?" I asked gently.

Mrs Marylebone didn't answer. Instead she pulled a framed photograph off the table next to her and pressed it into my hands.

"That's my Harry. He's in front of the shop there. See he's got the apron on, clean and tidy as ever." I squinted at a faded picture of a man in front of a grocer's shop. He was a big man with broad shoulders and a handlebar moustache.

"Now, Harry died nearly ten years ago. And is it right that someone can come along and accuse him of things and he isn't around to defend himself?" Pink spots had appeared in the old lady's cheeks.

"I'm still not sure what exactly your husband is being accused of."

"Harry and Reg had gone down to Cornwall together. It was a business thing, some trade show or another, I can't remember now. But they had some good weather and the two of them went for a swim. Only Reg swam out too far and Harry couldn't save him." Her words sounded like she'd said them a hundred times.

"Mrs Marylebone, is there something you're not telling me?"

"People talked. They said nasty things, even then. They said that maybe it wasn't an accident. They said that Reg had drowned and that Harry had held him under. Because Reg was sweet on me."

"And was he?"

"It was all so long ago? Does it even matter?" Mrs Marylebone buried her face in a white lace handkerchief, but I had seen her eyes for just a second. And I knew with complete certainty that she believed her husband had murdered Reginald Platt.

"You had a productive afternoon, then," Fort said as we walked to the home of Eliza Darlington.

"I should say so," I replied. "Sooner or later, I will connect the crimes mentioned in the letters and I will find their author." I sounded more confident than I was, but I did at least feel like I was getting somewhere. Unlike in our other case.

While we were waiting for a response from my letters of introduction to most of the Bloomsbury set, Fort had discovered that Miss Darlington worked just a few blocks from our office. We had decided to visit unannounced.

I had imagined a tiny garret in run-down boarding house, or perhaps an easel in a corner of a trendy café. What I hadn't expected was a former munitions warehouse near the river that had been turned into a huge open space full of artists.

We edged our way past metal sculptures that towered over us, piles of discarded canvases and strange exotic textiles. The artists themselves scurried about carrying paint or tools or merely sat contemplatively beside one of the large windows. I had been brought up on Victorian upper-class art – men on horseback and women in large hats – and there was something exhilarating about the displays, even if I didn't understand any of it. Eventually we were directed to a large space in the centre of the hall where there were large canvases dotted with geometric shapes and bold colours.

"Miss Darlington?"

The figure at the easel turned and revealed a woman in her early thirties, with a long, square face that was free from makeup. She wore paint-spattered overalls on top of her dress and she made sure to set her brush and easel down carefully before crossing the room to meet us.

"My name is Edward Moreton and this is my partner Charles Fort. We are here in connection with a missing manuscript, and we were hoping that you might be able to help us."

Darlington looked puzzled. "What manuscript?"

"The Intransigent Delphinium. By Mr Stephen O'Hendry."

The young woman laughed, then wiped roughly at a smear of paint on her cheek.

"Surely no one could care about such a thing apart from the author himself," she said, still smiling.

"You are aware of Mr O'Hendry's work?" I asked.

"The one that calls himself the Rake? I read a short story of his in 'Word and Art'. It was nothing but dreary people living dark little lives. Well, no one wants to read about that do they? I found him deeply depressing."

"O'Hendry told us that many of his fellow writers were jealous of his success."

"I believe he sold a fair few copies of his last book, but as I say, I haven't read it. Of course, if we measured success by how much money we made it would be a sad state for art, would it not?"

I took this to mean that Miss Darlington's own work was not a great seller.

"You didn't know O'Hendry personally?"

She looked at me sharply for a moment. "Clearly Stephen has already told you about me. Why not ask directly? Did I have a love affair with Stephen O'Hendry? Yes. It lasted barely a month. I thought he might be an interesting diversion, but it turns out he is just as dull as all the others."

Fort and I looked at one another. We had heard nothing of the kind. But it was useful information.

"Why did the affair end?"

"I told you: he bored me. And he was always in need of money for something or other. And I've got a bit of it. My father is one of the Darlingtons of Somerset, you see."

"You felt he was using you for money?"

"His family used to be rich, before he wasted it all. Problem is, he kept his expensive tastes without the means to get them."

"Didn't earn much money from his books then?"

"He did all right for a while, placed some stories in some big

55

magazines. But that sort of thing soon dries up. He was relying on this new book to dig him out of a hole."

"What will he do now?"

Darlington shrugged. "I suppose he will have to write another."

When we left the building it took several minutes before the scent of turpentine left my nostrils.

"What did you think of the paintings?" Fort asked.

I dodged around a pair of paint speckled artists to pull open the factory door. "Interesting, I suppose. A change from landscapes and portraits of dogs."

Fort grinned. "I like a little more feeling in my art. A bit more warmth. Miss Darlington was a rather chilly figure, don't you think?"

"Perhaps, but does that make her a thief?"

"Not necessarily. But I don't think she would hesitate, should she believe it necessary. People of her class are used to living beyond the law."

I turned to him with a raised eyebrow.

"Or working for it, of course," Fort added, "Do not be offended my friend. I just meant that she doesn't fear the consequences of her actions."

"Did you think that the paintings looked familiar?"

Fort nodded. "The same sort that were at O'Hendry's house. If it were such a brief relationship then why would he adorn his walls with her art?"

"Could we be looking at a jealous ex-lover?"

"If so then I'm afraid Miss Darlington moves to the top of our list of suspects."

Chapter 9

The rain came on just as we left Miss Darlington's studio. Fort and I hurried into a hansom cab.

"Where to now, Edward?"

I checked my notepad. "The offices of Cutler and Associates. Mr St. John Cutler is O'Hendry's publisher. And O'Hendry didn't seem to like him much."

"I'm afraid that authors and publishers rarely have much love for one another. One creates art, the other sells it. It can be a difficult combination." Fort had a look on his face which suggested he spoke from personal experience.

"If we are to believe O'Hendry then the publisher may be our top suspect, as your Sherlock Holmes might say."

I scratched my chin. "My money is on Miss Darlington. A love affair would be a better motive for the theft."

"But what of Worthing's list? Those literary worthies who have suffered loss to thievery? And the fact that they also appear on O'Hendry's list of possible perpetrators?"

I groaned. Fort could never accept a straightforward explanation. "I am not sure I follow."

"Neither am I," Fort grinned, "but I prefer the adventure of discovering a literary caper to a jealous girlfriend."

We arrived before long at the address of Cutler and Associates and climbed out of the cab into the afternoon drizzle. I had to check the address twice. The publisher's offices were sandwiched in between a firm of lawyers on the one side and a tobacconist on the other. Faded gilt lettering proclaimed the establishment's title next to a steep staircase up from street level.

We squeezed up the narrow staircase, climbing until we reached a long thin landing with a door at the end. There was a bell by the door, a tarnished nameplate and nothing else.

I rang the bell and waited for an age. Finally a short thin man with a monocle and a beard that flowed down to his waist opened the door.

"Don't tell me: you've written the greatest book on the planet and you want me to read it," the man said gruffly. He looked like some breed of elf that had got lost from a fairy tale by way of Bedlam. He spoke with a whistling sound that displayed a rather obvious lack of teeth.

"Nothing like that. We're government investigators and we've come because of Mr O'Hendry's missing manuscript."

A long hissing wheeze came from behind the beard and it took me a moment to realise that the man was laughing.

"I never thought that The Rake could cause me any more trouble. Guess I was wrong. Come in."

Cutler led us down a narrow corridor that was lined with books, all faintly mouldering into the walls.

"It's a bloody cave," Fort muttered behind me and I remembered that the American was claustrophobic. Finally the corridor opened onto a small office with a desk and a single chair.

"Where are your associates?"

Cutler frowned. "Oh, you mean the company name? Well, I had a secretary once but she didn't last long. No, I used a little literary license on that one."

In the absence of anywhere to sit Fort and I leaned against a heaving bookcase while Cutler sat down in a dust-smeared chair.

"So you're here about the missing manuscript. I must admit, when the Rake came and told me it had gone, I half thought he'd just asked someone else to publish it. Not that anyone else would be interested."

"You've read O'Hendry's book then?"

"Oh yes. His writing is just as awful as you might imagine. But with one exception: The Rake does have a rather beautiful way with parody. Honestly, I never knew he had it in him. So there are sections of the work that are written as pastiches of the hallowed Bloomsbury set. And those are rather fine."

"O'Hendry sends up his fellow authors?"

"Yes, and not with kindness." The man gave a wicked grin. "It's almost a diabolical gift."

I turned to Fort. "That might give us a motive. Perhaps a fellow author stole the manuscript to prevent embarrassment."

"Or an artist, or a critic," Cutler added, "half the establishment is in there somewhere."

"Are you?" Fort asked.

Cutler chuckled. "Of course. But I am well aware of my own foibles. It was rather amusing to see them written down in print."

"How did you come to be O'Hendry's publisher?"

"He had submitted a few shorts to some collections I edited. Nothing spectacular, but they were interesting for their raw, unpolished nature if nothing else. So, rather against my judgement, when O'Hendry asked me I agreed to publish

Delphinium. The thing is, despite his truly dreadful prose, the man does sell. He has created this Rake persona that tends to take the fancy of a certain type of bourgeois young lady. God knows why."

Fort flicked through a pile of paper samples. "And what does the missing manuscript mean for you, Mr Cutler."

Cutler frowned. "Well, it probably won't make much difference. At least I won't have to front up the advance. Publishing isn't quite the financial certainty that it once was."

I looked around the poky little office. "I never would have known."

Cutler glared. "One doesn't do it for the money, young man. One does it for the love. I once took tea with Tom Hardy while he tried to sell me one of his late novels and he spent the whole time talking about the curve of St Paul's dome. You don't get that working in a bank." The story had the stale air of the oft-told tale.

"Did you buy it?" I asked.

"Buy what?"

"The Hardy novel."

"Ah. Well, no. He wanted more than I had. It went on to do rather well." Cutler turned away with a grumble that might just have been, *bloody Far From the bloody Madding Crowd.*

"Well, I think we have everything we need for now," I said, with forced cheeriness and ushered Fort out of the room. We hurried outside to the fresh air.

"What a dismal little place," I said.

"Hardly the beating heart of London publishing," Fort agreed. "I wonder how bad his finances really are."

"And how the loss of O'Hendry's manuscript might affect them."

"Indeed. Will you join me for a drink?"

"I'm sorry Fort, I must head home. Important government business."

My reason for hurrying home was that I had arranged to spend an evening in the company of Victoria MacMillan, my neighbour and sometime girlfriend. Recently my relationship with Victoria had been crawling rather than racing along. I still held out hope however, even though she seemed to be cooling towards me. An exciting case to regale her with might just help my position.

I hoped that a literary caper might fit the bill, but as I told her about the missing manuscript and the strange goings on in Bloomsbury, Victoria seemed less than impressed.

"They should try living in the real world." She said when I told her about O'Hendry's pain at the loss of his manuscript.

"I suppose that he spent a lot of time writing it..." I found myself in the curious position of defending O'Hendry - and for the first time I felt genuinely sorry for the man. Yes, he had no knowledge of the real world, but didn't that mean that he was more likely to feel the pain of his loss?

I realised that I had not spoken for several minutes and Victoria was looking at me with a mildly irritated expression that I knew well.

"Sorry. It's just that the man has nothing else in his life. He calls himself the London Rake, says that he gets all these women throwing themselves at him, but if you saw him you'd know that that's as big a fiction as his books."

"He sounds like a prize imbecile to me," Victoria said, blowing smoke through her lips. She was standing next to the window so that some of the smoke was drawn out into the night. It would probably not fool the landlady: Mrs Davenport had strong views about ladies who smoked. I left the subject of O'Hendry and his problems. Victoria seemed unusually taciturn tonight and the author's story had annoyed her in a way I had not expected. I made my excuses and retreated to my room.

I arrived at the office the next morning to find Chief Inspector O'Connell waiting for me.

"I wanted to know how you got on with Mrs Marylebone."

I filled the policeman in with my meeting with the old woman. "It sounded to me like the letter writer might have a point about the young man's drowning."

"Well, we'll never prove it, with both men dead," O'Connell said with a resigned tone. "It is as we thought then. We appear to have a serial poison pen."

"What does that mean?"

"Well, it doesn't seem like the writer could be connected to your sister, Bishop Gaskell and to Mrs Marylebone. Instead it's just someone picking victims at random to cause trouble."

"Picked at random?" A voice boomed from the doorway. Charles Fort dropped into his chair. "My good man, randomness is the sister to coincidence. Both are weapons of the conventionalist, those who would prefer the banal explanation rather than searching for a higher truth."

"Mr Fort," O'Connell said with a weary edge to his voice, "I'm sure I don't understand half of what you say. Is this how all Americans speak?"

Fort's moustache bristled and I decided to interject.

"I think what my partner meant was that there must be some connection between the victims."

"I do not deny it. But it may be something so small that we should never discover it." O'Connell picked up his coat. "Don't get me wrong, I would love to see the author of these hateful things behind bars. But I do not have the resources to track down a thousand possible connections."

"Connections are our specialty," Fort said.

"Well then, I wish you the best of luck."

When the door shut behind the Chief Inspector I slumped down behind my desk.

"O'Connell has a point. I just don't see how an old lady like Mrs Marylebone and a woman like my sister can have angered the same person. It doesn't make sense."

"Well, why not consider that events that may seem disparate and disconnected might in fact be related?" Fort settled into his lecturing pose. "One favourite pastime of our scientists is to ignore the relation of earth to sky. One early example was the earthquake of 1661 where during the ground quakes monstrous flaming things were seen in the sky. But the disparate phenomena did not end there. It was reported that a Mrs Margaret Petmore went into labour and birthed three baby boys, all of which were born with a full set of teeth and the power of speech."

"Really?" I asked, rather horrified.

"So it is written. Why then does it confront our scientific sensibilities to consider that the abnormal in obstetrics and the unusual in terrestrics might be connected?"

Well, I had little to add to that, so I stayed silent.

"It seems to me," Fort continued, "that it might be time for us to spread ourselves a little further."

"What do you mean?"

"Your poison pen case and our work involving the authors of Bloomsbury are both becoming rather demanding. I think we should use our time more wisely to investigate all aspects of the cases. So I will take the investigation of the missing novel. You will assist of course with the tedious interviewing and evidence collection and so on, but I shall conduct all the research. You may keep the case of the anonymous letters."

"Are you sure, Fort?" In truth I was rather excited at the idea of leading my own investigation.

"You have followed my method for over a year now. Although I have much still to teach you, I believe you will be able to apply yourself admirably. With my supervision of course."

Not perhaps a ringing endorsement, but I felt myself swelling a little with pride.

"I'll do my best."

Chapter 10

I slept badly that night. For some reasons my dreams were beset by demonic babies who spoke incomprehensible philosophies in an American accent and smiled toothsome grins.

I awoke late and put on the little stove that I kept in my room to make some tea.

"Morning!" Liz walked in without knocking. I must have forgotten to lock the door. That wouldn't happen again.

"A little early isn't it?"

"Ah, humbug, you were always a tardy riser. Is that tea on the stove?"

I brought out another cup. Liz stared at the chipped stoneware with some surprise.

"How... rustic."

"I've been busy working on your anonymous letters," I explained while I made the tea. "It looks like the writer has sent them to several other people, including a Bishop and an old woman."

"Actually, that's just what I wanted to talk to you about," Liz said. She had just reached for her tea when there was a knock at the door.

"Just a minute." I opened the door to Victoria. She was holding an angry black cat.

"Take this for me," she said in a whisper, "I'm hiding him from Davenport." She pushed the cat into my arms before she noticed there was someone else in the room. Victoria's eyes ran over Liz, taking in the dress, the make-up, the immaculate coiffure.

"I'm sorry, I didn't realise I was interrupting something."

I gently pulled Victoria into my apartment with the hand that wasn't holding an angry feline.

"Miss MacMillan," I said formally, "I would like you to introduce Liz… my sister."

I watched a faint blush spread across Victoria's cheeks, followed by a smile.

"Oh, Miss Elizabeth. It is a pleasure to meet you."

"And you." Liz took Victoria's hand. "But please, call me Liz. You are a friend of my brother's so we are practically sisters already."

The two women looked each other over. I felt the back of my neck begin to perspire. I allowed the cat to leap from my arms and it immediately took up residence in the middle of my bed.

"How are you enjoying the Ministry?" Liz asked Victoria.

"Well, it's an interesting position. They sent me to Paris last year."

"How wonderful," Liz clapped her hands together in delight. "Paris! I went to finishing school in a darling little place just off the Champs Elysees. Mais avez vous essaye les macarons de la patisserie Stohrer?"

"I'm afraid I didn't pick up much of the language."

"Oh."

"I was just heading to the office," I said before the silence became too uncomfortable.

"Then I will walk with you," Liz said. "I hope we will meet again soon," she added to Victoria.

"As do I." Victoria turned to me. "I'll see you at dinner, Edward."

"Of course." As she left, I felt like there had been a hundred unspoken exchanges between the two women and I hadn't understood any of them.

We were barely out of the hallway before Liz pinched my arm. "I always wondered why you would live in such a dreadful place. Now I understand perfectly."

"Liz…" I said, my expression a warning.

"Please, don't worry, I'm leaving." She gave me a massive wink. I resisted the urge to kick her shin. I waited for a few moments while she hailed a hansom cab.

"About these letters, Liz."

"Oh, that's what I wanted to talk to you about. Listen, Eddie, I think it's best if you just forget about them."

"What?"

"Well, Henry and I talked it over, and the more attention gets drawn to this business the worse it could be for us. Henry was quite definite, I'm afraid. And you and your American friend are not exactly known for your discretion."

"But Liz, I really think that these letters might be dangerous. Three people that we know of have been targeted."

Liz gave a laugh that was a little forced. "Now you're being silly. I wish I had never told you about them in the first place. Some jealous wretch venting their spleen, that's all. I'm asking you Eddie, please let the matter drop."

I didn't have a chance to reply before she climbed into the waiting carriage and drove off.

"You are late this morning," Fort said mildly when I arrived at the office.

"A scenario involving two women and a black cat."

"Oh," Fort said, suddenly interested just as I slapped my hand to my forehead.

"Damn!"

"What is it?"

"I left the bloody cat in my room." I sat down behind my desk trying not to imagine just how much mess the creature might make by the time I went home. "Liz came to see me this morning."

"Did you ask if she had received any more letters?"

"I never got the chance. She asked me to stop investigating the letters. Practically begged, in fact."

Fort raised his eyebrows. "That is interesting. Did she say why?"

I shook my head. "Just that her fiancé had suggested it might cause more of a scandal if I tracked down the letter writer."

"He could be right."

"But that was true all along. Why would she suddenly change her mind now? I think this fiancé has influenced her."

"Have you met him?"

"No. But I certainly intend to now."

A young clerk put his head around the office door.

"Sir, I have some cards for you."

"Thank you. Look here, Fort," I said triumphantly once the man

69

left, "Mr and Mrs Leonard Woolf invite Lord Fotheringham and his associate to attend their residence at Tavistock Square. And there are others from Strachey and Simmonds."

"They are probably all hoping for a rich patron." Fort replied with a grumble.

"Well, no matter, at least we get to speak to them. Who should we see first?"

"The Woolfs," said Fort, "I rather liked her book of short stories."

"They are the ones with the Press?"

"Yes. They are the beating heart of the Bloomsbury set."

"Then off to Bloomsbury we go."

Tavistock Square was on the plainer strain of Georgian architecture. The Woolfs lived at number 52, occupying the first two floors. I rang the bell and a maid showed us upstairs.

"Welcome to our home." Mr Leonard Woolf stood in the centre of the room and introduced his wife who rose from her chair to greet us.

In appearance the Woolfs were rather well suited, both with long faces and straight noses. They might have modelled for a sculptor in ancient Greece.

"Please call me Virginia." I took Mrs Woolf's hand and looked into quite the saddest eyes I have ever seen. They stopped my tongue for a moment before I managed to stutter a greeting. Just as soon as she had spoken, she went back to her chair.

"I presume you are here about the Press," Leonard said, looking from myself to Fort. "You want to commission something?"

I shuffled my feet. "I'm afraid that is not quite the case. You see we are here on behalf of His Majesty's Government. We are investigating the left of a manuscript."

Leonard's face darkened. "Is this about that fool O'Hendry?"

"Now, dearest," Virginia said in a warning tone.

"Strachey told me yesterday that he's been going around the town ranting that someone stole his manuscript. He should be thanking them. London Rake indeed. He tried to take the dreadful thing to us, did he tell you that."

"He wanted you to print his manuscript?"

"That's right, with our Hogarth Press."

"And you weren't interested?"

"The thing was mostly mediocrity disguised as a sort of modern novel – all fragmented prose and interminable pauses. But the worst parts were the parodies of other writers. How he could take it here after what the damned book said about Virginia."

To my surprise the woman by the fire let out a cackling laugh.

"My husband feels that he must protect me. He is my knight gallant. But I am not so sensitive as he assumes. O'Hendry's prose did not hurt me. I found it rather amusing."

Leonard Woolf blushed and there was an awkward pause while the husband and wife looked at one another.

"May I ask who else O'Hendry attacked in the book?"

"Oh, the whole lot of us, what people like to call the Bloomsbury set." Mrs Woolf seemed irritated by the name. "No victim escaped the barbs of the Rake's pen."

"I don't suppose you are interested in our own act of vandalism?" Leonard Woolf asked.

I remembered belatedly that Worthing had mentioned other crimes among the literary elite. "Ah, yes, I believe there was something..."

"Half a dozen bottles of the finest purple ink. We use it for the marbled paper. It costs a bloody fortune and someone took it right out of our own basement. A deliberate act of sabotage."

"Or some petty act of theft," Mrs Woolf said idly. She rolled a cigarette by hand and lit it with an ember from the fire. She then sat back and smoked in her chair, as if she had tired of the conversation.

"Did you say purple ink?" Mr Woolf nodded and I looked over to Fort who gave a small nod. My friend had told me never to overlook a coincidence, and I couldn't help but be reminded of the violet scrawl of Liz's anonymous letter. Could there be a connection?

"Our assistant at the press noticed it. Here, I'll give you his address." Leonard Woolf went over to a large writing desk in the corner of the room and scribbled on an envelope.

I saw something on the desk that looked like a strange spiky modern sculpture. When I moved closer, I saw that it was a collection of pots stuffed to the top with pens.

"Ah," Virginia smiled from the armchair. "A little weakness of mine. Many a year I have spent searching for the perfect pen. The feel of it, the sensation in the hand... You understand I'm sure."

Fort nodded just as I shook my head. I looked again at the pens to see if I could see any traces of purple ink but there didn't seem to be any.

"Is there anything further?" Mr Woolf asked as I took the address from him. He seemed rather keen for Fort and I to leave, so we said goodbye to the couple.

"Rather a brusque individual," I said, thinking of Leonard Woolf as Fort and I made our way back to the office. "There was something about Mrs Woolf, though. Something... out of the ordinary." I wondered if it were the presence of artistic genius. Fort had given me some of her work to read but it wasn't really to my taste. Apart from some nice parts about dogs.

"Yes, as I said before I have often wondered if artists may not be closer to those wild talents that I am so interested in. Abilities that are so exceptional that they are outwith our understanding of the human."

I made a noncommittal noise. The woman had seemed almost unworldly, that was true. At the same time I liked her better than her husband. However, I couldn't imagine either of them creeping into O'Hendry's house and stealing his manuscript. So we were back to square one.

Chapter 11

"Is it still acceptable to drink sherry in the afternoon?" My landlady, Mrs Davenport, asked, with a coquettish smile. She had a powdered wig that towered over her and was wearing her Sunday best dress.

I was still not sure which occasion we were celebrating. The late Queen's anniversary? Some sort of War Memorial Day? No matter, Davenport had cornered me at lunch on Saturday and made me feel guilty until I agreed to come.

There were sandwiches and iced buns laid out for tea but they were at present covered with muslins and there was no sign of us being allowed to tuck in. I looked at them longingly and smiled when I caught Victoria doing the same.

"She snared you too then," I said as I followed Victoria to a sofa.

"'Fraid so. Couldn't think of an excuse fast enough. Plus, I'm trying to stay on her good side to stop her snooping about and finding Napoleon."

"Napoleon?"

"The cat."

"Ah," I said. The name suited him. When I had returned from work the night before I had been greeted by claw marks all over my room and the distinctive tang of cat urine. I had yanked the creature out from under the bed and deposited him with his contrite owner.

"Wouldn't you prefer a puppy," I remarked, remembering how the black creature had scraped its claws along my arm.

"I detest dogs."

"Really?"

"Dull things. And much too needy. Cats are so much more independent, don't you think?"

"Is that a good thing?"

Victoria gave me one of her unreadable looks. "I rather think so."

I took a sip of the sweet sherry. It reminded me of my grandmother. Still, it was good to see Davenport playing the gracious hostess. Since her recent courtship with Mr Smethwick – a grocer from Watford – had blossomed into an engagement, her catering had definitely improved. And Smethwick's cut-price produce probably helped ease the strain on her purse.

Smethwick himself was sat in the chair closest to the fire with Davenport fussing over him like a mother hen. The comparison was particularly apt as he was round with a bald head that did look rather like an egg. He caught my eye and winked at me. I quite liked the man.

We said a toast to the King and then, thankfully, we were allowed to eat. As I grabbed an egg sandwich, I felt a tug on my arm. It was Davenport's beau and he led me over to the fire.

"Saw you at the track last Sunday," Smethwick said in a low voice.

I started and looked around for Victoria. Thankfully she was at the other side of the room trying to look interested in Davenport's latest antique acquisition, a rather ugly Milton vase.

"I think you must be thinking of someone else," I said.

Smethwick snorted. "Someone else with a gleaming Silver

Ghost that goes like the clappers? I don't think so."

"All right. It was me. But I'm trying to keep it quiet so don't let on, will you?"

"I get it. Don't think your young lady would approve?"

"She's not my young lady."

Another snort. "But you'd like her to be, hmmn?"

"I couldn't say."

"Well, you certainly have more talent for cars than you do for winning over the ladies. I saw you give Windmore a run for his money."

Dash it all, I was rather flattered. "Well, the Sailor is still the best in the business, but I rather think his Austin is showing its years." There then followed a discussion between Smethwick and myself in hushed tones of the greatest racers at Brooklands. We had just begun to argue over the merits of American manufacturing when we saw Davenport turn our way.

"And that is why I think that Gilbert and Sullivan are still the best night at the theatre, don't you?" Mr Smethwick gave me a comedic wink.

"I agree entirely," I said.

"Ah, now, I have a soft spot for Oscar Asche." Mrs Davenport said, coming over to join Smethwick. "All those exotic costumes and colourful sets, it makes one long for the East."

I had never considered that Mrs Davenport might desire to see far off lands. She was growing more interesting by the day.

"If you'll excuse me a moment." I had spotted Victoria over by the door and I wanted to catch her before I left. I caught her eye and she gave that smile that lifted my heart. I decided to take a chance.

76

"I wondered if you might want to come to the car racing over at Brooklands with me next weekend."

"A car race?" Whatever Victoria had been expecting me to say, this was not it.

"Yes. It's rather fun."

Victoria looked at me, considering the idea. "I'm afraid it's not really my idea of fun, Edward. I wouldn't think all that smoke and noise would be yours either."

"Well, you never know until you try it. Let me know if you change your mind."

"It is time you put the young lady out of your head."

When I had met Fort the next morning in a rather melancholy mood, my friend had interrogated me until I confessed that my lack of progress with Victoria was becoming rather a sore point.

"Easier said than done, Fort."

"Well, I'm sure I have plenty of research for you to occupy yourself with. First off, I have some notes for you to catalogue on lost manuscripts."

With only a small sigh I sat down to work through accounts of Homer's *Margites* and the lost books of the bible. My interests piqued rather more with some clippings related to lost Shakespeare plays.

"Do you really think that *Cardenio* exists?"

"Ah, the lost Shakespeare. Well, the play was written, and it was performed. But since then it has disappeared from the earth. And so it joins the ranks of the lost."

"Maybe it's sitting on Cutler's shelves: there could be anything in there."

"It is a thought. Perhaps the lost play might be sitting in someone's attic. Or it has landed in some super Sargasso Sea where it will hover above us until the end of time. Or it may never have existed in the first place. History tells us it existed, but history is a dangerous mistress: one would be best not to trust her."

I decided it was time to get out of the office. "Would you like to come with me to Lytton Strachey?"

"Let me guess, somewhere near Kent?"

I wasn't entirely sure if Fort was joking. "I meant the critic. One of our suspects in the case of the stolen manuscript."

"Ah yes, Mr Strachey. Let's go."

Lytton Strachey was even slimmer than the Woolfs and I was beginning to wonder if any of the Bloomsbury set ever actually ate. He sipped on lemon tea and contemplated us through large glasses, stroking a long red beard. He looked like the archetypal scholar.

"This is a family place. I stay here when in London." We were in Hampstead in a beautiful white townhouse with pillars at the door. The room was tastefully furnished with some interesting nudes on the walls. Strachey, however, seemed a little ill at ease. His eyes flicked from Fort to me, and back again.

"We won't keep you for long, Mr Strachey. As I said, my partner, Mr Fort and I are working on an investigation for the government."

"Your name is familiar to me, Mr Fort."

"Oh, you may have heard of my novel, 'The Outcast

Manufacturers'?"

"I'm afraid not. Was there something else…"

"I have also found some fame with another book, 'The Book of the Damned'." It was rather strange to see Fort be humble. I had to work hard not to stare.

"Of course!" Strachey said. "I read it just last month. I found it thoroughly modern."

I wasn't sure if that was a compliment or not but Fort beamed with pleasure. I thought it wise to move on.

"We're here in connection with Mr O'Hendry's missing novel."

Strachey looked surprised. "Oh, really? I wouldn't have thought that a lost book by the Rake merited such a detailed investigation?"

"He apparently has some connection with the Deputy PM," I confided.

"Well, that explains that. Do you know, my first thought when I heard the book had disappeared was that he had stolen it himself?"

"Why would he do such a thing?"

"The Rake is what I consider to be the worst kind of poet. Just enough talent that some fool will always publish him, not enough to make him actually worth reading. And, like so many writers, his opinion of his work is much higher than anyone else's."

"Have you had run-ins with him before?"

"I published a piece about his poetry pamphlet in The Strand. It was, perhaps, not very flattering. But then, the job of the critic is not to flatter."

"And you would have no reason to steal the manuscript yourself?"

Strachey smiled. "I cannot conceive of one. I suppose if I got rid of it then I wouldn't have had to read the dreadful thing. But if I took the chance to destroy every bad book that crossed my path I would never be done."

"Did you know that he had written several parodies of Bloomsbury members in the book?"

"Did he indeed? Well, I suppose that might make it mildly more interesting."

"It might give one of them a motive to steal it."

"Or me, you mean. Perhaps if The Rake had been a better writer. But the book would have soon ended up in the mire of obscurity anyway. No, I don't think myself or my friends are to blame."

Strachey had relaxed now, his hands with their long, delicate fingers lay on the arms of the chair.

"Mr Strachey, if I may ask, why were you so uneasy when Fort and I first arrived."

Strachey looked twitchy. "I thought you might be here because of my... personal circumstances."

I found my eyes slip to the nudes on the wall. All of which were male.

"We are not here to investigate anyone's private lives, especially if it is not relevant to our case." I smiled, trying to put the poor man at ease.

"I am glad to hear it. With so many malicious busybodies about nowadays, one can never be too careful."

Fort and I left Strachey's in time to catch a train back into the town.

"Did you notice his boots?" Fort asked as we sat in the smoking carriage.

"No."

"Come now, Moreton, you must be more focused. The boots were old and scuffed. Country boots. This man is not normally resident in the city. Yet he appears just when O'Hendry's book disappears."

"Could be a coincidence?"

"Of course it could. But consider this: might the man's personal proclivities be just the sort of thing that O'Hendry might satirize in his book. That would give Strachey a reason to dispose of it."

I considered this. "Perhaps. But it just doesn't seem like it would be in the man's character."

"Or is it that you felt sorry for him?"

"I did feel sorry for him. He seemed like a gentleman. It seems unfortunate that his choice of lover might make him a target for others."

"Such is the way of the world, my friend. But we should not eliminate him from our list of suspects purely because we like him."

"True."

"And do not forget that he is a critic. They are one species that I would believe capable of anything."

Chapter 12

When I arrived at the office the next day, I found Charles Fort pouring a cup of tea for a large man with red whiskers and a broad back.

"Chief Inspector, have you any news on the anonymous letters?" I asked.

"I'm afraid I'm here on rather more serious business. Do you know a man called St John Cutler?"

I looked to Fort, waiting for him to enlighten O'Connell, but the American just shrugged.

"He is a publisher of novels. We went to see him two days ago," I explained, not surprised that Fort had already forgotten the man. "We're investigating a missing manuscript and Cutler was meant to publish it."

"This would be the manuscript of Stephen O'Hendry, also known as the London Rake?"

"Yes."

"Well, I'm sorry to inform you that Mr Cutler was found dead last night and we arrested Mr O'Hendry for his murder this morning."

"What, Cutler has been murdered? And you think O'Hendry did it?" I slumped into a chair. It was rather a lot of information to process in one go.

"Mr O'Hendry was found in the office standing over the dead man. Chap next door heard a commotion and caught him in the act. The body was still warm. Blow to the head, most likely, although we'll have to wait for the doctor to confirm it."

"And O'Hendry confessed?"

"He's not said anything yet. Well, nothing that makes any sense. The man was raving when we arrived. Quoting poetry. His own, I believe, judging by the laboured metaphors. He was intoxicated, or smelled like it at least. I've left him in the cells to sober up before we interview him."

"He didn't seem like a killer," I said. "What do you think, Fort?" The moment I spoke I knew it was a silly question.

"All appearances are illusions. No man who has ever looked down the sight of a microscope could possibly doubt it. To judge by what a man 'seems' to be is to jump to the kind of homogenous conclusion that the dedicated researcher must do without."

There was a pregnant pause. Fort coughed. "But to address the case at hand, no, I would not have pegged Mr O'Hendry for a killer. Besides, what had he to gain from the death of the only man willing to publish him?"

"Quite," O'Connell agreed. "But, with respect Mr Fort, there may be some motivation of which we are at present unaware. You'd be surprised the reasons that one man finds to do away with another. Or perhaps you wouldn't."

"One thing I don't understand," I interrupted, "Is how you knew that we had an interest in this case."

"Well, that was the other things I came to ask about. This was on his desk."

A torn off corner on an envelope on which was written: 'Moreton, Horse Guards, 831, London.'

"Why, that's the number for the office. How would he get that?"

"I assumed you gave it to him."

"No, I didn't. To be honest, I had found the man rather lacking in information." I experienced a moment of guilt. I had not felt that Cutler had much connection to the case of the missing manuscript. Perhaps I had been wrong.

O'Connell frowned. "So why would he want to contact you? Could he have remembered something relevant to your case?"

"Something about the missing manuscript?" I mused. "He never got the chance to tell us."

The Chief Inspector placed his hat back on his head. "So it comes back again to O'Hendry. Cutler must have remembered something important about the manuscript. Something that might have got the author in a bit of bother. Perhaps Cutler told the Rake he was going to tell you – well, whatever it was – and the young poet offed him there and then."

"Could be," I said.

"I can see you are still sceptical. Why don't you come and interview the man with me tomorrow morning? He should be ready to talk by then."

The afternoon was rather quieter as Fort ruled that we must not be distracted by the Inspector's visit.

"The clippings wait for no man, Edward. How are your investigations into the poison pen letters getting on?"

I handed Fort a sheaf of papers with more than a little pride. "I still think that I need to connect the victims to find out what Liz had in common with the others."

"A sensible strategy."

"It seems to me that I need to discover whether or not the

allegations in the letters are true. If I can find out who knew these secrets then I can discover the author of the letters."

Fort clapped a hand on my shoulder. "Excellent work."

"Thank you. So I have started with perhaps the most difficult case, that of the death of Reginald Platt." I fanned out the small collection of newspaper articles on the desk before me.

"First, there is the initial article on Platt's death. The local Morning Star newspaper describes it as a 'Tragic Drowning.'"

"Go on." Fort had leaned back in his chair and closed his eyes in what I hoped was concentration.

"Platt was pulled from the water by his friend Harold Marylebone. That's the old lady's husband. Now, the article says that even though he was dragged to shore Platt couldn't be revived."

"Anything else?"

"It says he left behind a sister and mother in Brighton."

"Aha!"

"Indeed. Two people with a motive to send the letter."

Fort's eyes snapped open. "But remember to look beyond the obvious. Yes, the sister and the mother would have reason to want revenge. But why now? Why so long after his death?"

I drummed my fingers on the desk. "Perhaps some of the other pieces can give us some information. Can we be certain that Mrs Marylebone's claim that her husband tried to save Platt is correct? Or is it like the letter writer said? Did he cause his death rather than attempt to prevent it?"

"Now, Edward," Fort wagged a finger at me. "Remember that the letter itself says nothing of the kind. It implies, for sure, but it does not actually state the libellous claim."

85

I pulled the letter from my pocket. "Some information has been given to me regarding the death of a Mr Reginald Platt in Cornwall in 1892. I know this will be of interest to you. Dash it, Fort, you're right. The letter never says that Mr Marylebone killed anyone."

"And so our letter writer proves to be of the most devious mind." Fort picked up his pipe and filled it carefully. "Once again, I am struck by the inconsistencies of these letters. The reticence in naming the crime seems almost overly cautious. Yet the clumsy request for money is something out of a third-rate novel."

I shrugged. I felt that Fort was rather over-egging the point. Did he really expect a poison pen writer to behave rationally?

"Here's an interesting piece," I passed a slip of paper over to my partner. "It's a follow-on item in the local paper a week after the Reginald Platt died. It says that the Chief Inspector in charge, name of Peterson, was looking for witnesses to the drowning. Do you think that means he had his suspicions?"

"Perhaps. Did he find any witnesses?"

"A few tourists saw Platt pulled from the water but none are named here."

"Hmmn. We are sorely lacking in data. The provincial press is not what it used to be. No hint of scandal or anything untoward." Fort shook his head sadly.

"I think I should concentrate on Platt's family."

"That seems logical." Fort had already turned back to his volumes of arcane wisdom. A little matter of an unexplained drowning could hardly hope to keep the interest of Mr Charles Fort for long.

"How is your case of the missing manuscript?" Victoria asked as she bit into a piece of bread and butter.

"I like that, it sounds rather like a Sherlock Holmes mystery," I replied while I passed her a bottle of lemonade. We had discovered a rather delightful picnic spot in the eaves of the attic space of Horse Guards Avenue. When it was sunny we could prop the tiny sash window open and dangle our legs out into the sunshine. Today, however, it poured. On the rare occasions where Victoria could steal a lunch break from the typing pool, we would meet like this. I liked the clandestine feel of our lunches. Victoria seemed to like them too.

"You would make a fine Watson," she said.

"What?" I said, genuinely horrified. "Surely I am Holmes, and Fort is my companion?"

Victoria gave a small, sideways smile. "As you wish. So is the game afoot, Mr Holmes?"

"Actually, it is rather more serious than that." St John Cutler's murder rather dampened the mood. I explained to Victoria that the Rake had been arrested for his death.

"Well, you didn't paint him to be a vicious murderer."

"That's just it. He didn't seem the type. And why would he murder the only person with any interest in publishing the damned book?"

"Perhaps he was getting revenge. Could Cutler have stolen the manuscript? Destroyed it even? Then this O'Hendry could have killed him in an artist's rage?"

I shook my head. "Why would Cutler have taken the manuscript? It's a possibility, I suppose, but I can't see why. Perhaps I'll learn more when we interview the Rake tomorrow."

Victoria kicked her shoes off and stretched her toes out. "Your job is so much more interesting than typing up memos."

"Really? You said just last week that it was policing for the privileged."

"Did I?"

"And that I was Fort's pet slave and that chasing spooks and ghouls was no occupation for a future lord of the realm."

"I can be a dreadful cat, can't I." She looked at me with those dark eyes. "I'm sorry. Truth is I'm jealous."

"Jealous?" I moved a little closer. Victoria bit her lip.

"When I came back from Paris I had this idea that everything would be different. You cannot imagine how wonderful it was in France. Everything new, everything exciting. But then to come back to London to my little job, my little flat, my little life…"

"You are bored," I said, rather abruptly. I was, of course, a part of that little life that she so despised.

"It's more than that. I want to mean something. I want my work to make a difference. Pah, you could never understand what it's like to be a woman like me."

There seemed little I could say to that so I let the silence linger a while.

"Have you read any Virginia Woolf?" I said finally.

Victoria laughed and hugged her knees. "Well, I didn't think you were going to say that. No, I haven't."

"I met her the other day. She was something rather special. Most of her work is beyond me. But I read 'The Voyage Out' and I think you would enjoy it."

"I would?"

"It's about… well, I suppose you could call it the discovery of the self. Or, rather, learning how to go where you should go. I'm not explaining it very well, but at the end of the book someone says: 'It's not cowardly to wish to live.'"

I stopped, a little embarrassed. Victoria stared up at me.

"That is quite beautiful." At that moment she leaned towards me and placed a hand on my chest. I ran my finger around the curve of her jaw to draw her face to mine.

The ear numbing toll of Big Ben struck the hour. The chime was echoed across the bells of Whitehall so sharply that Victoria and I sprung apart. We looked at one another for an awkward moment.

"Goodness, that's one o'clock. I must get back to work."

I watched her flee down the stairs. I brushed the crumbs from my shirt with a sigh. Back to work.

Chapter 13

I was finding it is very difficult not to smack Stephen O'Hendry in the mouth.

"I don't see why I should speak to the police. They are the epitome of tyranny by the state."

The London Rake appeared to have suddenly become a Bolshevik. I didn't remember him feeling quite so anti-establishment when I was paying for his tea and scones at the Russell Hotel.

"Now, lad," Chief Inspector O'Connell never seemed to lose his patience, despite his suspect's lack of cooperation. "I'm no tyrant, despite what my constables might say behind my back. Why don't you just tell us how you came to be in the room with the dead man?"

"I told you a hundred times, I don't remember how I got there. First thing I knew about it was the shopkeeper grabbing me and screaming for the police. That's all I have to say."

O'Hendry's feet tapped the floor in a nervous percussion. I caught Fort's eye and found his exasperated expression mirrored my own. O'Hendry was scared, that was very clear, but if he was innocent then he couldn't be making a worse effort to defend himself. The thing was, for some reason I believed him.

"Could I have a word with the gentleman alone?" I asked.

O'Connell raised his eyebrows. "If you can talk some sense into him, then sure." The Inspector rose and gestured to the constable at the door and my partner to follow him. The door shut behind them with a loud clang.

"You're not helping yourself, you know, talking like that to the Inspector."

"Aren't I?" the Rake buried his head in his hands. "What's the point anyway, they've already made their minds up. It'll be the courtroom for me next. Maybe I can write a new Ballad of Reading Gaol."

I leaned across the desk and grabbed O'Hendry's lapels. He shrank backward with a yelp.

"Now listen here, boy. Prison is not a romantic place. It is not inspirational, or any other artistic nonsense. It is a miserable place for miserable people, so don't be getting any notions otherwise. You need to show the Chief Inspector that you're innocent."

O'Hendry sniffed and turned his face towards the wall. I decided to try another tack.

"Of course, who's to say you'll end up in a cell at all, even if they do find you guilty?"

"What do you mean?"

"I mean a carefully planned murder of a frail old man? Who's to say that you won't end up at the end of a gibbet?"

Finally this seemed to have some impact. The Rake's face lost its confident sneer.

"They wouldn't hang me."

"You sure about that? Sure enough to risk your life on some foolish notion?"

The Rake bit his lip and shuffled his scuffed black shoes. I sat down on the edge of the table.

"Tell me what happened."

"I had a telegram from Cutler. It was in the morning, said he wanted to see me. But I had already made arrangements with some friends so I didn't get to the office until the evening."

"And you were drunk."

"A bottle of Absinthe. It does wonders for the creative mind, you know."

"I'm sure. And your drinking buddies?"

The Rake frowned. "Some old friends from Cambridge. I can give you their names. And Eliza. She'll always appear if there's the prospect of a hearty drink."

The name was familiar. "Eliza Darlington? The artist? Wasn't she on your list of suspects for the theft of the manuscript?"

O'Hendry glared up at me. "Well, shouldn't one keep one's enemies close? Besides, perhaps I was wrong about her. She doesn't have the brains to think up something as sly as that. Old Simmonds was at the party too, you looked him up yet?"

I checked my notebook. "You mean Mr Francis Simmonds? He was on your list too."

O'Hendry tapped his nose in a rather pathetic attempt to look wily. "Keep your enemies close…" he repeated.

"Right. And you went for a drink in…"

"The Lamb on Conduit Street. A few ales with lunch then back to Simmonds's place where I am afraid I rather overdid the Absinthe. It does so get the creative juices flowing."

I wasn't convinced. I was not much enamoured of the green fairy myself, having tried an illicit cupful at boarding school and been royally sick.

"When did you turn up at Cutler's office?"

"That's just it, I can't remember. I don't even remember leaving Simmonds's tawdry little flat. I remember sitting drinking by the fire, then next thing I know there's people shouting and a dead old man on the floor. Listen, Moreton," O'Hendry looked at me, his expression wretched. "You've got to get me out of this mess."

"If you're innocent then you must trust in the system. The Inspector will not hang an innocent man."

O'Hendry snorted and made an obscene gesture with his fist which told me exactly what he thought of that idea.

"So what did the Rake tell you?" O'Connell was in his office, feet up on his desk. Fort was examining a shelf of books with a dissatisfied expression.

"He spent the day of the murder getting drunk with his friends. Absinthe."

O'Connell tutted rather primly.

"Sounds like he barely knew his own name after a couple of hours, let alone being able to kill anyone," I explained. "He's scared, but I don't think he's guilty."

"Unfortunately what you think won't mean much to the jury," the Chief Inspector said. "Come now, Moreton, give me something I can use."

I sighed. "The man is a buffoon. His politics are all over the place. Liberal one minute, Bolshevik the next. I can't see him having the gumption to murder Cutler."

"So you've said," said O'Connell

"Have you any other suspects?" I asked.

"Cutler lived alone in a one bedroom flat that was even more run down than his office. His landlady said he never had any visitors and spent all the daylight hours at his office. He didn't know enough people for there to be many suspects."

"So O'Hendry is your only possibility." I still couldn't help but feel that the Rake was innocent.

"Unless you gentlemen can convince me otherwise, I'll be charging him tomorrow."

O'Connell showed Fort and me to the door.

"Where do we begin, Fort?" I asked as we walked down the steps of the police station.

Fort brushed the ends of his moustache with his little finger. "The scientists always begin with definitions. But nothing has ever been defined because there is nothing to define. Like looking for a needle that no one lost, in a haystack that has never existed. But that element of searching, the striving for definition itself may be a thing."

"Fort, you are quoting yourself again."

"Am I? Ah well, what I mean is that we must look beyond O'Connell's definitions of 'suspect' and 'victim'. Consider what we are truly looking for, and we may find illumination from the search itself."

"I think I'll call it a day," I said, checking my watch. "I am getting a headache."

I awoke to a dreadful hammering on the door of my apartment. Still half asleep, I pulled on some clothes.

"Coming!" I shouted and lurched to the door. I just had time to open it before the man broke through it.

He came at me with fists flying. He was bigger than me, with a dark complexion and he was shouting something unintelligible as he came.

On instinct, I dove to the side and let him crash into the room. He righted himself and with a bellow like an angry bear he ran towards me again. This time he caught me a blow on my arm before I could pull out of the way.

The pain barely registered until after I let my own fist fly. I connected with the man's jaw and he went down in an instant. He grunted in pain on the floor and a planted my foot on his back to make sure he couldn't move.

"Mr Moreton, what in heaven's name is going on?"

Mrs Davenport stood with her hair in curlers and her face red with anger. "Never, in all my time as a landlady…"

"Important government business," I cried as I hastily pulled the door closed. I could still hear her shrieking through the woodwork.

The man had struggled onto all fours and was rubbing his chin. He caught sight of me and gave another roar.

"Enough," I said. "I don't know who you are but if you come at me once more I will have to hurt you."

Finally some sense seemed to cut through to the man and he sat back down.

"You caught me off guard," he mumbled.

"Who are you?"

I could see the fire still flickered in the man's eyes. He certainly had a dangerous aspect to him. "Someone that is concerned with a lady's honour. Which is more than you are, you blackguard."

I thought for a moment. Some paramour of Victoria's? I hoped not but it might be possible. Then I looked again at the man's swarthy appearance. Realization dawned.

"You must be Liz's beloved Henry."

Another bellow as Fashton rose to his feet. "How dare you speak her name!"

I moved back a little. The man had taken leave of his senses. I didn't doubt I could beat him, but I didn't think Liz would appreciate that.

"I am not who you think I am," I said, edging away until my back was against the wall.

"I saw you with her. She came to this dirty little place. You have bewitched her with your common ways, you cad!"

The man looked up at me with a baleful expression. He wore an expensive hand-made suit. He also smelt of expensive whiskey. It was so strong that he might have been bathing in it.

"I am her brother, you fool."

"Don't talk such nonsense. Liz's brother is the heir to the Dukedom. He would hardly live in such a cesspit as this."

"You better hope my landlady didn't hear that or we'll both be out on the street." I sighed and walked over to my bureau. I grabbed a card and threw it over to the young man.

"To my darling Eddie on your birthday," Henry read, "from your favourite sister, Liz. Ah."

"Ah indeed. So you believe me now?"

"It is Elizabeth's handwriting." The young man was beginning to calm down. I hadn't realised how tense I was until I started to relax. Now I was just moderately angry.

"You have been a prize arse," I said.

"Well, I was protecting a lady's honour." The bluster was beginning to fall away from the man and he looked rather sheepish. I gestured to an armchair.

"You had better sit down and catch your breath."

"Thanks. That was some punch."

"Try any more nonsense and I'll give you another."

Fashton held his hands up in a gesture of peace. "I'm done, I swear." Now that I could see him in the firelight I didn't much like the look of him. The combination of his swarthy complexion and his pomaded hair gave him a greasy appearance. And his suit was altogether too fashionable. He looked like a man desperate to fit in. Which meant he probably never would.

"I'll make some coffee," I said and lit my stove.

"Why does this place smell of cat?"

"Just be quiet and tell me why you're here."

Chapter 14

"All a misunderstanding," Henry Fashton said, his large hands cupped around his steaming coffee. He had drunk his first cup so quickly he must have burned his throat, then asked for a second. At least he was sobering up.

"Well, why don't you explain exactly what you misunderstood?"

Fashton cracked his knuckles. "How was I to know that you would live in such a…" He looked around the room with vague disgust.

"Compact space?"

"Quite. My man told me that Liz came here yesterday. He saw you leave together. Well, what was I to think?"

"Hold on," I said, "what do you mean your man saw us?"

"Eric, an old friend of mine. I'd asked him to keep an eye on Liz."

"You were having my sister followed?"

"For her own protection! I was worried about the letters, that someone might mean her harm."

I leaned forward. "Liz told me you asked her to stop the investigation into the letters. Why would you do that if you wanted to protect her?"

"She said that?" The man frowned. "I don't understand, I never asked her to stop the investigation. I was damned glad when she said she'd asked you to look into them, even with your reputation."

"My reputation?"

Fashton laughed and some of the colour came back into his cheeks. "Well, I don't mean anything by it, but your present... career is a bit of a talking point in our circles. An Earl who spends his day either in the library or chasing around spooks and spectres." Fashton snorted into his coffee. "We've even got a name for you."

"Really," I said calmly, "what is it?"

"Liz calls you the Monk."

"Does she now."

The man met my eyes and his face fell. "Now, old chap, it's just a little joke. Liz thinks the world of you."

"Then why did she tell me to stop investigating the letters?"

"I have no idea. All I know is that it didn't come from me."

Fashton's mood had darkened. He threw back the last of his coffee and stood up.

"I am serious about your sister. I plan to marry her. There are not many women that would turn that down. You might remind her of that when you see her next."

I had no intention of becoming my sister's matchmaker. "She has agreed to the engagement, has she not?"

"Yes, but the secrecy, and now these letters... She would do well to mind her place." With that, Henry Fashton jammed his hat on his head and slammed the door behind him.

I poured the coffee remnants down the sink. What could Liz possibly see in such an oaf? Was it just the money? The title? Or was there something I was missing.

"I'm glad you're here, we have work to do." It was past nine

99

and I was still half asleep. Fort moved energetically around his study, pulling books from the shelves and placing them on the already teetering piles on his desk.

"Tea?" Anna asked, sticking her head around the door.

"No, thank you, too much coffee today already."

"You look a little peaky, Edward," Fort said, peering at me through his spectacles.

"I had an early morning visitor. The Honourable Henry Fashton, who was not in the mood to behave honourably."

"The meeting did not go well?"

"Not exactly. He did say something strange though. He said he didn't ask Liz to tell me to stop the investigation. So it must have been her idea."

Fort put down the book he was holding. "Why do you think she would do such a thing?"

"I don't know, but I intend to ask her as soon as possible."

"Good idea. Do not leave off your inquiring spirit just because the case deals with family. In our profession, it is every thinker for himself. But for now we must consider the unfortunate demise of Mr Cutler."

"Have there been any developments?"

"Chief Inspector O'Connell telephoned to say that the post mortem would be carried out today. I have arranged to meet Mr Simmonds in a public house in an hour."

"Who is Mr Simmonds again?"

"Really, Edward, have you not been keeping up with your notes? Simmonds is an author, one of the names on O'Hendry's list of suspects for the theft of the manuscript."

"Then let's go and see him." I massaged the bruise that Fashton had left on my side. "I could do with a drink."

Mr Simmonds had started without us. His corpulent figure was balanced precariously on a wooden stool at the bar. It was early and there was no one else there.

"Mr Simmonds, the author?" I asked. It was a safe assumption as he had several notebooks and quills scattered over the bar counter in front of him.

"Ah, a fan of my work?" Simmonds accent veered from a faint Midlands tone to well-to-do London. "Well, I suppose I can spare a few moments to talk about my latest novel..."

"Not exactly. My name is Edward Moreton, and I am investigating Mr Stephen O'Hendry's lost manuscript. This is my partner, Mr Charles Fort."

"Charmed," Simmonds said, giving a smile that exposed some yellowing teeth. "But doesn't the Rake have more than a missing novel to worry about? Word is that he's in prison for bashing his publisher's brains out."

Fort and I exchanged a look. "I was not aware that that was public knowledge."

"News travels fast in the literary world. Authors are dreadful gossips. Worse than fishwives."

"So you believe that O'Hendry killed Mr Cutler?"

"Is there some doubt in the matter?" Simmonds raised an eyebrow.

"Too early to tell," I said vaguely.

"Well, I must admit I was rather taken aback when I heard. The always Rake seemed to be all talk. I couldn't ever imagine him actually getting his hands dirty."

"Did you know Mr Cutler?"

"Know him?" Simmonds gave a snort. "We weren't exactly good pals, but yes, I knew him. I saw him on Tuesday morning as a matter of fact."

I nearly choked on my pint. "He was killed that afternoon. What did you see him for?"

"Business, of course. The money-grabbing scoundrel. Yes, I knew him and I will not mourn his passing. Not one little bit."

When Simmonds leaned forward to drink from his glass his large stomach protruded against the edge of the bar. His face spoke of a man who was no stranger to this position. I set down my beer and wished I had ordered a half.

"Could you tell me about your meeting with the publisher?" Fort said, peering at Simmonds's notebooks.

"I arrived at half past ten. The lazy cretin was still in his housecoat. I do believe he slept in that office half the time. I always thought it would be his lungs that did for him in the end. Who would have thought he would end up as something as interesting as a murder victim?"

"And you were there to talk business?"

"My war memoirs. I was in the artillery division. Fought in more battles than most. The first volume was published last spring, and it was a great success if I do say so myself. Perhaps you have read it?"

"I don't think so," I said.

"Well, Cutler had an option on the second volume. Just a formality, really, when the first had been such a success. But he said he wasn't interested."

A touch of red crept across Simmonds's cheeks. "It was preposterous. And I told him so."

"So you and Cutler argued."

A large vein began to throb on the author's temple.

"Damn right we argued. He told me that his press wouldn't take the book. Despite everything I've done for him. I mean, had he forgotten that 'The First Ache' sold fourteen thousand copies? Of course he had read that blasted article in the Strand."

"What article?"

Simmonds fished inside his jacket pocket and brought out a newspaper cutting which he thrust across the bar.

"Last Tuesday's piece in the literature section. You must be the only man in London who hasn't read it. Spiteful little thing, written by Mr Bloom S Bury." He snorted and gestured to the barman for another drink while I scanned the well-thumbed piece of paper.

I found the article largely incomprehensible. There were multiple jibes at an author who was 'passed before he had arrived' that I could only assume from his irate expression referred to Mr Simmonds.

"Character assassination," Simmonds explained when I looked at him in confusion. "I wrote a novel a few years back that did rather well. And then I wrote my memoirs. The article accuses me of jumping on the bandwagon, of writing what sells, not what actually matters."

"And worse than that," Fort said, his eyes scanning the page, "the article implies that the war actions you recounted were not your own."

"Spotted that did you? Yes, it basically accuses me of faking the whole thing. Would I have sold eighteen thousand of them if they weren't true?"

Fort set the cutting down on the bar where Simmonds stared at it as if it was about to catch fire.

"Do you know who wrote the article?"

"A few names sprang to mind, but even if she didn't write it herself I bet I know who's behind it." He was looking positively manic now and slammed his hands on the table with increasing force. "I sent her my latest novel, but the old hag simply won't let it pass."

"Old hag?"

"Virginia Woolf, Stephens as used to be. A dreary thing, even as a girl. And she runs the press, whatever Leonard may tell himself. And old friends are cast out the door. Did I mention that 'The First Ache' sold twenty-three thousand copies?"

"You did. Do you really think that Mrs Woolf would have written such a thing?" I thought back to the lady with the solemn face. It hardly seemed likely.

"Oh, they love their japes, the precious Bloomsburys. Just like that Dreadnought business. No doubt she thought it would be amusing to see me dissected in the paper. No matter, the readers shall decide."

Simmonds turned back to one of his notebooks and began scribbling furiously.

"One more thing," I said as I pulled on my overcoat. "O'Hendry said that he was at a party at your home on the afternoon of Cutler's death."

Simmonds nodded slowly. "Yes, I suppose it must have been

104

the same day. I invited some friends and some... acquaintances around to celebrate my birthday. Hardly a bacchanalian affair, but it was rather jolly."

"O'Hendry told us he was rather the worse for drink."

Simmonds chuckled. "The Rake was trying to impress the women, as ever. Started knocking back the absinthe like there was no tomorrow. He barely knew his own name by the time I kicked him out of the flat. Now I do have rather a lot of writing to do today..."

Fort and I took the hint and made our escape.

Chapter 15

"There may be hope for O'Hendry still," I said to Fort as we made our way back to the office. "Simmonds's account seems to agree with O'Hendry that he was in such a state he might have forgotten what happened on the day of Cutler's death."

"Perhaps, but this does not mean the man is innocent."

I considered this. Could O'Hendry have killed Cutler in a drunken rage then forgotten all about it? How would one ever prove such a thing?

"Do you think Simmonds truly believes that Mrs Woolf has a vendetta against him?" I asked Fort, keen to move to a less troubling line of inquiry.

"His artistic image has been wounded," Fort replied as he turned towards Horse Guards Avenue, "he is looking for retaliation. Still, someone wrote the article."

"I can't see a connection to Cutler."

"Connections are not always immediately apparent, my friend. A thing occurs, then another, but the relation between the two things may not be immediately clear. We have laid before us the murder of Mr Cutler. And Mr Simmonds's visit to see him earlier that day. The connection here is clear, but may be nothing. Someone writes a vitriolic attack of Simmonds in the newspaper. Is this third event connected also? Who can say?"

I sighed. "So what do we do with these unconnected events?"

Fort slapped my shoulder. "What the good researcher always

does, my friend. We take notes, lots of notes, and wait for enlightenment to occur."

"What I don't understand," I said, wanting to return our conversation to the case at hand, "is why Simmonds was so eager to be published by the Woolfs after they had made it so clear they couldn't stand him."

Fort ran his fingers absentmindedly along the edge of his moustache. "All writers crave the acceptance of their peers."

"They are like children, squabbling with one another and getting upset when they are not allowed to join the gang."

"Aren't we all?"

Belatedly I remembered Fort's proud expression whenever he saw a copy of 'The Book of the Damned'. I changed the subject.

"Do you think that whoever killed Cutler was the same person that stole O'Hendry's manuscript?" I felt that they must be connected, yet we still seemed to be missing the link. It was infuriating but Fort merely shrugged.

"Perhaps. I am not, as you know, a believer in coincidence."

An hour later and I was still mulling over the probability of O'Hendry's appearance next to the dead body being nothing more than coincidence. It was possible, but convincing the Chief Inspector would be a difficult task.

"Some correspondence for you, Mr Moreton."

I took the letters from the young lad and sat back down at my desk. Fort had made some excuse about research and had taken a trip to the British Library. The American had never entirely become comfortable with working for the War Office, even if they did pay his wages.

I flicked through the letters and stopped at one with a Portsmouth postmark. I slit open the top and read the contents.

Dear Moreton,

How's the Ghost? I won't be at the track for a few weeks, doing some teaching at the academy down here. Tell the boys to keep that garage tidy for me.

That name we discussed, I ran it by a few contacts of mine. It seems that the gentleman has been running up some debts. Loans unrepaid and so on. Could be getting rather sticky for him soon. Last seen in London a week ago, and it looks like he's gone to ground. Lot of people eager to catch up with him, if you see what I mean.

Hope this helps,

The Sailor.

I folded the letter carefully back inside its envelope. It was time to speak to Liz.

At that moment, however, Fort pushed the door open with an armful of books.

"A hand please, Edward." I leaped up and grabbed them before they fell to the floor. Fort flopped down onto his chair.

"Are these all relevant to Mr Cutler's death?" I asked. The

books were on subjects ranging from occultism in Imperial China to Renaissance religious architecture.

"Everything is relevant, and nothing is," Fort said. I narrowed my eyes.

"Besides," Fort continued, "I am dealing with the research in chronological order. Therefore I am staying focussed on Mr O'Hendry's missing manuscript."

"Don't you think we should try to discover Cutler's murderer so that we may clear O'Hendry's name?"

"I believe in the oneness of all things. When we discover the whereabouts of the manuscript, we shall discover our murderer."

"I admire your confidence," I said, while considering if Fort might have nipped into the nearest public house on his way back from the library.

"You will see that the books I have borrowed from the library are concerned with the phenomenon of teleportation. That is, an item that disappears from one place only to reappear in the next."

"I have heard you mention the term."

"I'm glad to hear you were paying attention. I have come across some new accounts of weird rains in these works that I have yet to examine."

I groaned at the mention of Fort's pet subject.

"Surely the lost manuscript can have nothing to do with weird rains, unless the pages have been falling from the skies."

"Try to imagine the bigger picture. What is a weird rain if not an object – many objects, in fact – that is out of place."

I sat back in my chair and folded my arms. While Fort gave yet another lecture on weird rains, I tried to imagine what to say to Liz, what questions to ask her. She was my sister, yet in the past few days I felt like I hardly knew her at all. I had just begun to drift off to sleep when a phrase caused me to sit bolt upright.

"What did you say?"

Fort smiled knowingly. "I said, my inattentive friend, that once upon a time there was a rain of virgins." The American gave a chuckle at my incredulous face. "In France a decade ago there was the singular anomaly of a shower of large hailstones, upon some of which were printed representations of the Virgin of the Hermits."

"That wasn't exactly what I thought you meant," I replied, settling back into my chair.

"Indeed, but doesn't it still strike you as fascinating. An anomaly apparently without precedent. But what if we consider the wider picture, quite literally. While the Virgin hailstones may be unique, there are many documented occurrences of pictures appearing in strange places. Women's faces, religious icons and so on have appeared on window panes. Not to mention the current fashion for strange appearances on photographic plates."

"And the relevance of this to our case..."

"Is not to view events in isolation. A hail of virgins seems unique, but once one puts it in context it is less so. The strange may be allayed with the ordinary. I believe that this is the case

110

for our current investigations. We have only to find the common ground, then all will become clear."

I sincerely hoped my friend was right. So far solving the murder seemed as likely as being hit by a virgin hailstone.

Chief O'Connell arrived after lunch with the autopsy report.

"Nothing paranormal about this one, I'm afraid," he said as he passed the papers to my partner.

"Death occurred by blunt force to the cranium," Fort read out. "How disappointingly banal."

"A crime of opportunity then?" I asked.

"Could be," said O'Connell. "A paperweight next to the body was smeared with blood, so it's a likely weapon. No fingerprints, unfortunately."

"And you still think O'Hendry did it?"

O'Connell shrugged, an impressive sight by six and a half feet of Irishman. "Motive, opportunities and the means. I have to say it is not looking good for your friend."

"O'Hendry is not my friend," I said.

"Then why are you so convinced he is innocent?"

I looked to Fort who merely raised his eyebrows.

"He just doesn't seem the type," I replied, somewhat lamely.

"All evidences of guilt can just as easily be evidences of innocence," Fort said. I chose to believe he was trying to

111

support my statement. O'Connell looked nonplussed.

"Well, Mr Fort, you will forgive me if I disagree with you on that one."

Soon after the Chief Inspector left, we had another visitor, one who declined to knock.

"What in God's name are you doing to free poor Stephen?"

"Miss Darlington!" She pushed into the office like a Fury on her way to battle. She had even rolled up her sleeves.

"Who else would it be? I have just been to see Stephen in the cells. He's having a dreadful time of it. He's even taken to writing poetry. Poetry! Of course it is woeful stuff. The bad poet is usually unconscious where he ought to be conscious, and conscious where he ought to be unconscious. Well, I wished he was unconscious after reading some of that drivel."

Fort put down the book he was reading and carefully marked his place with a notecard.

"You do not believe he killed Mr Cutler, then?"

"Cutler?   The man probably keeled over from gout, or emphysema or some terrible disease caused by lack of sunlight."

"Unlikely," I said calmly. "He was beaten over the head."

Miss Darlington paused. She looked at me down her long nose as if deciding if I was being serious.

"He was really murdered then?"

"So the police believe. And Stephen O'Hendry is their only suspect."

"Well, it is simply impossible. Stephen couldn't kill anyone, he wouldn't have the gumption."

I privately agreed.

"Murder?" Eliza Darlington pulled at the fingers of her gloves. "It can't be."

"I assure you it is so." I was beginning to find her refusal to accept the facts rather irritating. Her lips were set in a thin determined line.

"It must be a mistake. Even the police can make mistakes. I should know, my father was a policeman. He was a great man, but not infallible."

"And how are you, Miss Darlington?" The fire had gone out of her now and she was looking almost queasy.

"Oh, busy, always busy." She looked around the room as if she had forgotten why she had come here. "Listen, you must sort out this mess with Stephen. It simply cannot continue."

"If there is anything you know that can help clear his name then you must tell us, Miss Darlington," Fort said in a soft voice.

For a moment I thought she might say something, but then she gave a small shudder. "No, no, nothing like that. There is nothing I can do to help Stephen. It is up to you. You must save him."

Chapter 16

"Just how exactly are we going to clear O'Hendry's name? We haven't the faintest idea where to start."

After our visit from Miss Darlington we had retired to a public house just along the road in the shadow of the clock tower.

"Do not despair, Edward. If the man they call The Rake is as innocent as you believe then the research will support it."

"Do you really believe that?"

Fort pulled on the end of his moustache. "Of course. Although the interpretation of the research is always the difficult part. Convincing the good Chief Inspector will be the challenge. He demands hard facts."

"And where do you think the facts point?"

"Ah, I offer no opinion of the facts, I merely state them as plainly as possible. Let others infer causation or coincidence."

"Humph." I looked down at the dregs of my beer. "It just all seems so unlikely. Cutler was an old man who slept in his office. O'Hendry wrote a book that only a handful of people would have read anyway. How can these be high enough stakes for murder?"

Fort frowned. "You are correct, Edward. So instead consider for whom those stakes are the highest. Who do these events really matter to?"

"I'm not sure."

"Then find out."

It took me most of the day to track down Liz. I had telephoned my father's house – posing as a society columnist – but the housekeeper told me she hadn't been there for a week.

At last I turned up unannounced at the flat she kept in Piccadilly.

"Edward, wonderful to see you." Her face told me otherwise. "You should have called."

"I did," I said, following my sister into the large drawing room. The sun streamed in the window, warming up the air. "Several times, in fact. Your maid told me you were out."

I selected a large armchair in the baroque style and sat down. It was incredibly uncomfortable.

"I didn't realise I had to be constantly available," Liz said with a sigh. There were dark rings around her eyes but I was in no mood to be sympathetic.

"I met your fiancé. The man is an idiot."

Liz sat down in front of a large writing bureau. She picked up a poor attempt at some article of embroidery. "Well, he didn't like you much either."

"He told you he came to my apartment?"

"Yes."

"I don't suppose he mentioned he nearly beat me to a pulp."

"Actually, he said that you were more than a match for him. I'm sorry that he came to see you. Rather silly of him."

"Silly? Liz, the man tried to murder me!"

"You know Eddie, I'm not sure that this job isn't making you rather over-dramatic. It was all a misunderstanding."

I scowled. "Liz, you got me into this business and so far it has

115

been nothing but trouble."

"Then drop it. God knows, I've asked you enough times to let it go."

"Why? Why are you so keen for me to forget all about the letters?"

Liz looked out of the window. It was infuriating. My sister had her flaws but she had never been reluctant to speak before.

"Mickey Colton came to see me," she said softly.

"The man you told me was in South America?"

"That's where he said he was going. When he turned up last week, he said he had had a change of plans. And he needed some money."

Liz glared up at me, daring me to say something. But what was the point? She knew what I thought anyway.

"Did you give him it?"

"No. I swear I didn't. Even though he was in fear for his life."

"He said that?"

"He owed money to some bad men. That's how he put it. But I knew that Henry really would leave me this time if I gave Mickey the loan. So I sent him away."

"And he went just like that."

Liz grimaced. "He wasn't happy, but yes, he did."

"Did he confess to writing the letters?"

"Not in so many words. But I could tell. Men are so simple to read, don't you think? He had that guilty look that a dog gets when it has messed on the carpet."

"You didn't confront him?"

"What would be the point?"

I ran my hands through my hair in exasperation. "The point? So that we might find out more about the letters. It's not just you, Liz, what about all the other people that he wrote to, don't they deserve an explanation?"

Liz put down her needle. "I'm afraid that didn't occur to me."

A shrill ringing came from down the hall.

"Hold on a second, Edward. The maid is at the shop so I'll have to get that." And she hurried out of the room. I waited until the door closed behind her before I sprang up and began rifling through her desk drawers. I felt like I did when I was seven and I had read her diary.

I couldn't find anything of interest among the papers that littered the desk. I had half hoped for some familiar purple ink but there was nothing. I did find some rather expensive jewellery, still in the Harrods boxes. Gifts from Henry, I assumed.

The sound of footsteps echoed along the corridor and I quickly tied the desk. I was back in my seat by the time the door opened.

"Edward," Liz said and when I saw the look on her face my insides froze. "It's father."

Chapter 17

"I have never suited mourning," Liz said. She picked at a loose thread on the sleeve of her coat.

We were sitting in the back of one of the family's carriages. It was dreadfully old-fashioned but I had decided that the Ghost might not have quite the gravity for the occasion.

"At least it's not raining," I said, peering up into the clear blue sky. "We'll be at the graveside for at least an hour. The Archbishop is a dreadful bore."

"Don't let mother here you say that," Liz warned, "she used all her contacts to get him to speak. Rather a coup for father."

"He would have enjoyed that," I said.

"Now, Edward, don't be unkind. Not today."

I sat back against the leather seat and closed my eyes. The last few days had been draining. The arrangements were long and complicated. It was bad enough to have to deal with the formalities without having to pretend that I was grief-stricken. I had no idea what I was, but I certainly wasn't that.

"We're here," the coachman called as we slowed to a stop.

St Paul's Cathedral was at its most majestic, the great dome towering up into the sky. I got out of the coach and offered Liz my arm.

How strange to be at one's own father's funeral and hardly know a soul there. But that was the way of the aristocracy. The entire set turned out for each formal occasion. It didn't matter whose name was on the slab. As I looked at one grey face after another, I wondered if any were truly his friends. I had never met any of them. In fact, I wasn't sure my father had any friends.

The service was long and the cathedral was cold. I was all too aware of the eyes of strangers upon me. I looked at my feet. I didn't relish the attention.

Liz stared straight ahead and I wondered what she was thinking. I had let my interrogation of my sister drop when we heard about my father's death, but I knew I still needed to find out the truth about the anonymous letters. A voice inside my head whispered that I was distracting myself from the solemn occasion in front of me but I ignored it.

"It is your duty to take care of your sister now." My mother had appeared beside me without a sound. Rather like a vampire, I thought, then felt guilty about it.

"I will do my best."

"She needs your help. She is not as strong as she appears. We must protect her."

I was surprised at the vehemence in my mother's voice, but when I turned to question her she had already moved on.

After the funeral we took the carriage up to the hilltop cemetery that was the preserve of the richest families in London. There was a crowd waiting at the gates to the cemetery. Thankfully most of the people from the Cathedral had not made the journey to the graveside.

I spotted Fort and Anna standing awkwardly at the back of the crowd. I managed to manoeuvre my way towards them.

"Thank you for coming," I said. Anna patted my arm gently and gave me a small smile. Fort clasped my shoulder.

"Hang on in there, it'll be over soon enough," he whispered into my ear. I nodded.

My mother, smaller than usual in her black coat and hat, came over and pressed her bony fingers into arm.

"It was a lovely sermon, don't you think?"

I murmured assent. "Mother, this is Mr Charles Fort and his wife Anna."

She managed a grim smile and shook their hands. "I have heard so much about you, Mr Fort."

There was a long pause where no one quite knew what to say. I resisted the urge to stare at my mother. I had no wish to see her expression while she tried to place my companion.

"I'm sorry for your loss," Fort said solemnly. I took my mother's arm and manoeuvred her away from the American.

The walk to the graveside was chilling. In spite of the cloudless sky, the day had grown cold and the first strands of sunset were edging across the sky.

"Dust to dust," the Archbishop intoned, and I felt both my mother and sister shudder as the clods hit the top of the coffin. It was done. After the obligatory handshakes I made my way back to Fort and Anna.

A rumble of voices drifted across the graveyard. I could see some sort of commotion outside the gates.

"What's that?" I asked.

Fort frowned and peered through his spectacles. "I think it's the gutter press."

I grimaced. "That's all we need."

I thought of poor dead St John Cutler. Surely the press would be better spending their time covering his murder than

120

harassing the mourners at a funeral.

I took my mother's arm on one side and Liz's on the other. We swept past the men in felt caps as quickly as possible. A few of them murmured condolences while noting down our expressions on their notebooks.

I elbowed past a particularly obnoxious, weasel-faced man who grabbed my shoulder.

"How does it feel to be the Duke of Bentham?"

To that, I had no answer. I ducked my head down and entered the carriage, glad to be heading back to the city.

"Stephen O'Hendry has been charged with murder."

I looked at the Chief Inspector with bleary eyes. I hadn't slept well since the funeral and this was the worst possible news.

"I still don't think he did it."

"I know. But unless Mr Fort and yourself can provide us with some real evidence, there's nothing I can do. Where is Fort today?"

I frowned. "Late."

"Probably out chasing banshees or will o' the wisps."

"Probably."

"I'm sorry about your father," the Chief Inspector said, turning his hat around in his hands.

"Thank you."

At that moment the door to the office banged open.

"All hail the Duke," a bedraggled figure cried as it stumbled into the room, "and a merry afternoon one and all."

121

"Oh God," I said as I noted the beer stink that emanated from every pore of Charles Fort's body.

"Mr Fort?" The Chief Inspector looked rather taken aback. He had not been party to one of Fort's drinking bouts. I, on the other hand, had.

"Now, now, Fort, does Anna know what a state you've gotten yourself into," I said. I may even have wagged my finger at him.

"Anna? She's probably looking out the best China. How does one entertain the aristocracy? Come now, Chief Inspector, aren't you going to curtsy to the Duke?"

Fort dropped to his knees in an absurd pose.

"Perhaps you should leave us for the moment, Chief Inspector," I said and O'Connell fled gratefully from the room.

Fort had managed to drag himself over to his chair and slumped in it abjectly.

"Never in my life did I think I would have to play second fiddle to a Duke," he said morosely. I couldn't help but smile. How quickly the temper of a drunk could change. Now his mood seemed very black. "Have you handed in your resignation yet?"

"My resignation?"

"Wouldn't it be better to just get it over with?"

"What on earth are you talking about, Fort."

Fort raised his eyes to meet mine and I saw tears glistened in their corners.

"You cannot do this job and be a Duke."

I stared back at him. Of course, I had known where the conversation was headed but to hear it stated in such plain terms was like a dagger in my side.

"I can, Charles. I would not give up this life for anything." I knew that I had never spoken truer words.

"So you're going to what, abdicate?"

I grinned. "I'm not the King, Fort."

"Then what?"

"It is perfectly possible to be a Duke and carry out a career. In fact, in this century it is positively encouraged. I admit, the choice of vocation is generally rather different..."

"Wasn't your father head of the Admiralty?"

"Nonetheless," I continued, determinedly, "I see no reason to give up my position here."

Fort harrumphed in his chair. "We'll see. And how do I address the Duke of Kent when I want him to bring me a coffee?"

"Well, technically..." I paused.

"Out with it!"

"The correct mode of address would be 'Your Grace'."

Chapter 18

"I'm freezing my ass off, Your Grace," Charles Fort said, burrowing his neck deeper into his scarf.

I grinned but said nothing. Fort's hangover had well and truly kicked in and I had seen him in sunnier moods.

A particularly noxious London fog was in evidence. It sucked the heat from the sun and gave the buildings a faded, ghostly quality.

"Give me a rain of fish any day," Fort muttered as we hurried through the grey air, "anything is better than these damned pea-soupers."

I nodded agreement, not wishing to open my mouth to speak. The atmosphere felt distinctly unpleasant when inhaled through the mouth.

"And why are we out in this demoniacal weather?" Fort grumbled.

"Just before I heard that my father... Well, before we became distracted by other events, Liz told me that Mickey Colton had all but confessed to writing her the letter."

"Then surely we should let the Constabulary deal with him? I have a collection of sightings of Australian venomous mammals that I could be cataloguing."

I shook my head stubbornly. "We need to speak to the man. If only to rule him out of the investigation. I can go alone."

Fort grimaced. "I think I could do with the walk. My head is still rather tender."

We fell silent on the journey to the docks. It was not just the fog that dampened my spirits. My conversation with Hankey still haunted my thoughts. I knew I would have to tell Fort what our superior had said, only I couldn't find the words to do it.

"Is this the place?" Fort's voice was more than a little disgusted. I could hardly blame him. We had indeed reached our destination and it was a miserable outfit altogether. The rather grandly named 'Prospect of Whitby' had certainly seen better days. The pub had been around since the sixteenth century, and it looked like the décor hadn't changed much since. The fog of pipe tobacco was only slightly preferable to the noxious atmosphere outside. But at least there was a roaring fire to take the chill out of the air.

A group of men passed some well-used bank notes to one another, along with some envelopes of a substance that probably would have been of interest to Chief Inspector O'Connell. I looked away, not wanting to catch their attention.

Towards the back of the public lounge there were some women of questionable virtue sitting at one of the window tables, looking bored while their elderly male paramours played cards.

I took off my coat and commandeered the table nearest to the fire. I had to steer a still-gawping Fort to his seat.

"It's like something out of Dickens," he mumbled, and I couldn't help but agree. Dark twisted wooden tables, pock-marked mirrors and a disturbingly sticky floor. A nefarious place indeed, and just the sort of establishment where one might find a man such as Mickey Colton.

"Tell me again why you think our naval friend will be here?" Fort muttered, his eyes on the murky pint the barmaid had deposited in front of him.

"A tip-off." The Sailor had sent a telegram to the office with only the name of the tavern and a time: two o'clock. I checked my watch: it was almost a quarter to the hour. I sipped my half of ale. It was just as warm as I had feared.

A little too close to two o'clock exactly for it to be coincidental, the door opened and a group of men entered the bar. They were dressed in scruffy greatcoats and mud-coated boots that suggested they might work at the nearby docks.

I watched discretely as they ordered their drinks. Fort hadn't noticed them. He had brought out a copy of Euclid's Optics and was making copious notes in the margins. Good. I didn't want any of the American's distractions at the moment.

I tried to work out which of the men might be Colton, but they were all much the same age and colouring. Reluctantly, I rose from my chair and approached the men. Their group fell silent as I approached and I knew that they were silently appraising my expensive suit and polished shoes.

"Hello gentlemen. I wonder if you could help me. I'm looking for a Mr Michael Colton."

"Who?"

The pub seemed to fall silent. I swallowed.

"Mickey Colton. I've been told that this is his local. I would like to -"

I felt rather than heard the man approach behind me. I grabbed a bottle from the bar and spun around, keeping my centre of gravity low.

The punch that had been aimed for my chin went wild. As I wobbled and tried to stay on my feet, I realised that I was facing a giant. In fact, I barely came up to the man's chest. He must have arrived after his friends, because I certainly couldn't have missed him. He had to be six and a half feet tall, wearing oily overalls and sporting long black beard.

I just had time to take in these details before the man swung at me again. His technique had little finesse, but then it didn't need it.

I staggered backward against the bar. The group of men laughed and jeered and pushed their colleague towards me. Out of the corner of my eye I saw Fort carefully putting away his book. I waited for assistance, but my friend didn't seem in any rush to enter the fray.

"Stop!" I shouted rather pathetically as the man kicked out with one of his boots, catching me an agonising blow on the shin. I yelled and pushed my way along the bar. The whole place was roaring with laughter and jeers. At least I was providing some entertainment.

I still had the bottle in my right hand, but I was loathed to use it unless I had to. There was always a chance the bottle would shatter and cut the man to pieces. I didn't want to kill him, after all. It would be more paperwork than I could bear.

With a grunt of effort the big man came towards me once more. I raised the beer bottle, hesitated, then grabbed a shot of whiskey someone had abandoned on the bar. I flung it into the man's eyes and as he screamed I pulled back my fist.

It was like thumping a sandbag. I wondered for a moment if I had broken my knuckles. Somehow I had connected with his jaw hard enough to knock him out, if the earthquake tremor of him hitting the floor was anything to go by.

Fort sauntered over, pint still in hand and we both looked down at the man. The crowd fell eerily silent.

"Mickey Colton?" The giant was face down in the sawdust that covered the floor.

127

The door to the bar slammed shut. Fort and I looked at one another for a second, then we sprinted out onto the street.

A figure was disappearing into the fog. I forced my battered body onwards.

I had nearly caught up to the blighter when my knee gave way. That kick from the giant had been harder than I thought. The last thing I saw was Charles Fort puffing past me.

That's it, I thought, we've lost him. Then I heard a cry up ahead. I hobbled along the street until I found a curious scene.

A young man was face down on the cobbles with Charles Fort's boot firmly planted on his face.

"However did you catch him?" I wheezed to Fort.

"The technique of the ancient mystics." Fort grinned and smoothed down his slightly ruffled moustache. "Remind me to show you it one day."

"You'll be Colton then," I said as Fort lifted his boot. A handsome, if rather gaunt face looked up at us. "Why did you set your big friend on me?"

Mickey Colton got to his feet and glared at us both. "Don't like when fellows I don't know start asking after me. Gerry knows how to deal with any flash jobs that come sniffing around. Knock the other guy out before he has a chance to do you one. It's always been my motto."

"Rather easier as well if you've got a mate to throw the punches." I wondered if the giant had come around yet. At least I had left him still breathing.

"Think I'm going to risk my pretty face now, do you?"

If my knuckles hadn't been sore already I would have jabbed him in the eye.

128

Colton crossed his arms. "Just who sent a pair of Toffs like you anyhow?"

I narrowed my eyes. "I'm Liz's brother."

His jaw fell open. Then he smirked. "You'll be the Earl then?"

"Duke now," Fort said morosely. I ignored them both.

"Liz told me about the letters you sent."

"Didn't send any letters."

My patience was wearing thin. "The police are well aware of your little blackmail scam."

Colton scowled. "You've got no proof of nothing. Look, I like your sister. We had a little fun. Or should I say a lot of fun."

I took a step towards him just as Fort put his hand on my shoulder. I let the rage pass. Colton watched this with an amused expression.

"Look, I'm no fool. I knew it was just a short time deal. Just like she did. So maybe I asked her for a bit of cash. I was in a bind. But I never sent her no letters."

He was lying, I was sure of it. But there was nothing I could do.

"We'll be back," I said.

"You can't pin anything on me," Colton said. He shrugged off my arm and strode off along the street. I glared at him, but there seemed little point in following. The man was determined not to give any more away.

"Well, that was a complete waste of time," Fort said, smoothing down his coat.

I sighed. I could hardly disagree. I rubbed my bruised knuckles. "We must try again. We have to find out what's going on. Not just for Liz. Think about all the others."

129

"Then what do you suggest?"

I considered the problem for a moment, then smiled. "I think we need the female touch."

I left Fort to take a cab to his lodgings and hurried back to the office. I wanted to collect my notes on the case. If I was going to have a friend look over them, then I needed to get my own thoughts in order.

I was just shoving the files into my briefcase when there was a knock at the door.

"May I come in?"

Maurice Hankey, the most important man in the British civil service, made his way into the room. I pulled at my tie which had gone rather askew.

"Of course, Sir. Do you wish to sit down?" I tried to clear Fort's chair which was at present filled with a pile of insect specimens. Hankey, thankfully, chose to remain standing.

"I have come to offer my condolences."

"Ah." I tried to keep my face neutral. I was already finding that playing the part of the grieving son was... uncomfortable. "Thank you, Sir."

"I knew your father from the Club."

"Mmn." I didn't ask which club. It hardly mattered: my father had been a member of just about all of them.

"He will be sorely missed."

I dearly hoped that this awkward conversation would be over soon. I resisted the urge to look at my watch.

Hankey, to his credit, looked just as discomfited by the need for small talk. "And when will you be taking up your position?"

For a wild second I thought the man was offering me a promotion. "What position?"

"Well, you are a Peer of the Realm."

"To be honest, I hadn't really considered it. I will ensure that nothing much will change. I am still committed to my work."

Hankey chuckled. "Of course, you will keep your little hobbies. But I would rather like to know when you intend to vacate this office. I could do with another room for the press corps."

I began to grind my teeth. "I am serious, Sir. I intend to stay in my position, whatever my inheritance might be."

Hankey folded his arms. "I'm sorry, Moreton, but it is simply impossible. One cannot be a Lord and work for the service. Finish the cases that you are currently deployed on, if you wish. But after that you must clear out your desk."

Behind my back my hands balled into fists.

"All right, Sir," I said through gritted teeth. "Just give me time to break it to Fort."

Hankey shrugged. "As you wish."

The door closed behind my superior and an eerie calm befell me. I had known the moment I had seen Liz's face, I just hadn't wanted to admit it. It was hopeless, then. Everything was finished. But if I was to leave the service, I would at least close this final case. A few more days would make little difference in the end. I just had to hope I would find Cutler's murderer and the anonymous letter writer before then.

It was time to call for reinforcements.

Chapter 19

Only an hour later I found myself in the company of an attractive woman holding a pair of stockings. But perhaps not in the way that I might have hoped.

Renie Brien was beautiful, clever and irrepressible. The young American had travelled to London to become Fort's disciple. She was a student of Fort's phenomenological approach and had spent years studying just the sort of arcane occurrences that Fort bored me about daily. Out of a rather naïve sense of finding a kindred spirit, she had taken the boat to London in hope of becoming Fort's assistant. Only to find that the position was already filled. By yours truly.

I couldn't help but admire the woman. Having found her mentor rather disappointing in the flesh, she could have returned to her native land an embarrassment. But not Renie.

Instead, she had decided to embrace London and that city had had little choice in the matter. Renie was what every British person most feared and most admired about the Americans. Fort, I had soon realised, was an anomaly. He was quiet, studious, unassuming. Renie was the opposite. She was bright, loud, and unafraid of being the centre of attention. She was also ambitious, intelligent and had an excellent head for business.

So it had not been altogether surprising that within a few months Renie had set up shop in Covent Garden. She had opened an exclusive boutique that sold American fashion, including many of the little luxuries that had been unavailable to British women during the war.

"The Germans may never have taken Paris," Renie said as she folded a pair of stockings and delicately pushed them into a small cardboard box. "But they practically destroyed the clothes industry. Women want Parisian style, but they simply cannot get that at the moment. So they look to New York instead."

I stood awkwardly with my hands shoved into my pockets. I tried not to look too bewildered by the clothes in the shop. It was a far cry from the fashions of my childhood. Even Liz had never gone without a corset and elaborate skirts. Yet now young women were wearing outfits that would have been considered indecent a few years before. It was exhilarating and terrifying.

Renie pulled a striped skirt from a rack. "Victoria would adore this, you know."

Around a month ago I had introduced Renie to Victoria. Victoria loved her instantly. The two had been inseparable since. I was still regretting the decision.

"I'm not sure she would appreciate the gift."

"Oh dear, have you had a row?"

"No," I said, aware that I sounded like a grumpy child. "She just seems rather busy at present."

Renie gave me a wide grin. "Now Edward, you simply must try harder you know. Victoria won't wait around forever."

"Look, Renie, I'm here on business," I said, putting all thoughts of Victoria to one side. "I know you're busy but I wondered if you could spare a little time for your other occupation."

Renie scowled for a moment, thwarted in her attempt to engage me in a discussion of my sorry love life. "All right," she said. She called a young assistant out of the back to mind the shop and led me up a narrow flight of stairs.

"I tried to give it all up when I bought the shop," Renie said as she fished around in her apron pockets finally bringing out a heavy iron key, "but there's something about the work that gets into your soul."

The door opened onto a long room with low ceilings. The windows were lacking curtains so light flooded in to illuminate a wall covered in paper. Each scrap cut from a newspaper or magazine detailed some kind of anomalous phenomena. I recognised many from my own studies. Just like in Fort's house there were papers everywhere, although Renie at least seemed to be rather better organised.

I thought, not for the first time, that Renie would have made a much better partner for Fort than I did. At least in terms of her scholarship. I liked to think I had other skills that sometimes proved useful.

"Come and sit down." There was a comfortable chair next to a painted wooden desk and I sat down while Renie pulled up a second chair. Suddenly she grabbed my hand.

"Been brawling have we?" She said, turning my hand over to examine my bruised knuckles.

"Not exactly," I said, pulling it gently away from her.

"I hope you don't expect me to fight your battles for you?"

"Fort and I are investigating two separate crimes," I explained. "So between us we're rather overrun. I thought you might be able to help."

"Would this work be remunerated at all?" Turning shopkeeper had brought out a mercantile streak in the young American.

"Not in monetary terms. However..." I pulled a brown paper package from my satchel.

Renie opened it with an excited gasp. "'New Lands' by Charles Fort. Oh my goodness!"

"An advance copy. It won't be out until at least next year. But Fort said he would value your feedback." This was not strictly true. I had persuaded Fort to part with one of his precious proof copies to get Renie on our side. He had agreed only reluctantly. His feelings about his young admirer were somewhat ambivalent.

Renie's eyes glittered with excitement. "What do you need me to do? Is it ghost sightings? Vampires?"

"Not quite. I need you to invite a young man to dinner."

If I had been a more sensitive soul, I would have shrivelled up and expired under Renie's stare.

"He's a suspect in a case I'm working on." I filled Renie in about the threatening letters. "I'm afraid that this Michael Colton sounds like a scoundrel of the worst sort, but I want you to find out for yourself. I need you to find out why he wrote the letters. And how he got his information on the other victims."

"So you want me to seduce him?"

"I'm sure he won't stand a chance."

Renie smiled. "Well, it's not my usual sort of assignment, but I guess it could be fun."

I handed her a piece of paper. "He's working at the docks. The fruit warehouse, by all account. And I have his home address and his description." This last had been acquired by a judicial shilling note placed into the hand of the barman from the 'Prospect of Whitby'. "Perhaps you could wait for him outside his lodgings. Drop a glove or something."

"I'm sure I don't need your help to ask a man out for a date."

135

"Of course," I blushed. "Just be careful. If he is involved with these letters then he could be dangerous."

"Isn't everyone?"

Chapter 20

I left Renie Brien's shop hoping that I hadn't just thrown the young woman to the wolves. Or wolf, in this case. But while I was convinced that Mickey Colton was a cad of the first order, I didn't really believe he was a danger to women. Apart from to their reputation, of course.

A chill wind stung the back of my neck and I turned up the collar of my coat. Hankey's face when he told me to vacate the office kept rising unbidden in my mind. I felt like a clock was ticking away the seconds of the life I had chosen. But I knew I was fighting the inevitable. One could not escape one's breeding, no matter how hard one tried.

I found myself on the bank of the Thames. I looked down into its murky depths. If I had been one of the Woolfs – or even perhaps the foolish O'Hendry – I might have seen some sort of enlightenment. A metaphor for my hopeless condition, perhaps. But all I saw was murky brown water and a mud-splattered seagull.

"It's Mr Moreton, isn't it?"

Lytton Strachey was easily recognisable with his narrow frame and long beard. He came to stand beside me at the railings.

"That's right," I said. "Rather a cold day for a stroll."

The author bowed his head. "I grew up in a house full of children. I still find myself seeking quiet where I can. Are you the same?"

I laughed. "A little noise might have been welcome in my home. My father disapproved of noise. And children in general, I suspect." My voice caught in my throat. I should have kept silent. The man was technically a suspect in our case after all. But there was something about Strachey that invited confidences.

"Perhaps we always desire the opposite to what we have," Strachey murmured, his hands resting on his chest.

A thought struck me. "You haven't received any malicious letters, have you?"

Strachey's face was solemn. "What do you mean?"

"A number of people have been targeted by letters sent anonymously. I thought that perhaps you might have received one."

"May I ask what the letters contain?"

"Veiled threats to reveal secrets of the addressee. The usual nasty things."

"And you imagined that I might be a target for such a person?"

I felt rather like I was wading through the Thames. "If someone wanted to expose some... personal elements of your life."

The critic's mouth turned up at one corner. "My friends are well aware of my circumstances. I shouldn't think anyone would care."

"Your employers might," I persisted.

"Perhaps. But it is the twenties, Mr Fort. I have few secrets that would interest anyone who has not shared my bed."

For all my liberal ideas, I felt myself blushing. "I hope not, Mr Strachey. But if you do receive a letter..."

"Then I shall be in touch. Au revoir, Mr Moreton."

I hurried around to Fort's house. I needed to speak to the

American about the death of Cutler. I was in danger of disappearing into my own gloom. I needed to regain a sense of action.

"Ah, Charles, could you help me up?"

Charles Fort stretched out his right hand. He was lying fully prone on the floor of his study. Surrounding him were all the glasses and teacups from the cupboards, each filled with several inches of water.

I helped him up. Once upright he staggered slightly and I realised my friend was nearly stupefied from drink.

"My experiments have been less than fruitful," he said.

"Experiments? I thought you were going to research our missing manuscript."

Fort bent down and began to pick up the cups. I feared that not all of Anna's china would survive the process, so I began to help him.

"Oh, I was, I was... But I remembered a paper I had come across on the possibility of human levitation."

"Levitation?" I began to grind my teeth.

"The art of flying. I have read of Buddhist monks that were able to achieve such a feat. I thought I would give it a try."

"And the water?"

"I thought that if my body began to vibrate with a motion to small to detect then the drops might spill, proving that I had indeed moved upwards." He looked around a little crestfallen. "Thus far the floor remains dry."

"And what of our case, Fort?"

"Hmmn?"

139

I bunched my fists in frustration. "The missing manuscript? The death of the publisher?"

"Ah. I have been thinking about it, of course. But sometimes it helps to distract the body when the mind is occupied. In this way one might reach enlightenment."

"But Fort —"

The American held up a single digit. "You know not to rush my methods, Moreton. Youthful impatience will do you no good. I rather thought you had grown out of such things since our collaboration."

"I rather thought you had grown out of the brandy," I hissed.

Fort took a step backward as if I had hit him. "What has got into you, Edward?"

I just shook my head. "I will see you in the office tomorrow," I said, barely keeping the tremor from my voice.

Chapter 21

My mood could hardly have been more bleak as I hurried home from Fort's house. I shouldn't have been surprised that the man was having another episode of drinking. After all, it wasn't the first time. But the timing was unfortunate and I was feeling singularly low on patience.

I kicked at a loose cobble as I stomped along the street. I could hardly blame Fort for not appreciating the urgency of the situation. I had not yet gathered the courage to tell him that our partnership would soon be ending. Could he have guessed that I would not be allowed to work much longer? But whether he was aware of my situation or not, we still had a murderer on the loose. One might have thought that he would be trying a little harder.

I needed to get the American out of my mind. As it happened, I was passing a flower stall kept by an eager-eyed woman with a colourful shawl. I stopped and paid an extortionate amount to purchase a small bouquet of cheerful yellow irises. I grasped the paper wrapping and held them by my side as I walked towards home. I imagined that they might be a sword, protecting me against a faceless enemy. I brandished them at a baby in a perambulator who rewarded me with a sweet laugh. His mother pushed past rather quickly.

A wave of tiredness washed over me. Was this grief? This oscillation between melancholy and hilarity? The hand that clenched the bouquet felt clammy and cold. The scent of the flowers began to irritate my sinuses. Just what the hell was I doing? Running away from my problems as usual, my father might have said. He was dead, but that didn't make his opinions disappear. Would I ever be free from that life?

I thought of Fort, soaking in his bottle of brandy and pity merged with my irritation. If the American was falling apart now how much worse would he be when I announced the end of our partnership? Would I have to have his pain on my conscience along with everything else?

I had been walking without thinking and I found myself in front of the office of Mr Cutler and Associates. There was a note tacked to the door to say that all information on the death of St John Cutler should be directed to the local police station.

"Oi!" A lanky police constable appeared beside me brandishing a truncheon. "What do you think you're doing?"

I blushed in spite of myself. "My name is Edward Moreton," I explained and reached into my pocket to find my ministry pass. "I am a friend of Chief Inspector O'Connell's."

"Oh, you're the young Lord ain't you? He said you might be by. I'm here to keep an eye on things, only I had to nip around to the local conveniences if you get my meaning."

"All right if I have a look around?" I asked. The young man nodded and unlocked the door. He hurried up the steps in front of me, looking around to see if I had followed. I thought the poor fellow must have been terribly bored.

He hesitated in front of Cutler's office door.

"I'm sure the Chief Inspector won't mind you letting me in," I said, my fingers crossed behind my back.

The Constable turned around and his horse-shaped face was pale. "It's not that, sir. Someone's jimmied the lock."

I peered around the policeman and saw the splintered wood that indicated foul play.

"We better get inside then," I said. The young man nodded and brought out a heavy truncheon.

"Stay behind me," he said, rather unnecessarily as I had no intention of being anywhere else.

It only took a few moments for us to realise that the offices of the late Mr Cutler were empty. They had also been utterly ransacked. Papers were strewn everywhere, pages ripped from books littered the floor like a desiccated forest.

"Blooming heck," the policeman said as he shuffled through the debris. "How will we work out what's missing?"

I had been considering the same problem. The robbery, whoever they may be, could have removed anything they liked from the shelves and we would never be any the wiser. I slumped against the wall, feeling dreadfully sorry for the publisher. What a way to treat the man's life work.

"Any ideas who did this?" The Constable asked once he had blown his whistle.

"I'm afraid not," I replied. Had the murderer come back to find something he missed? Could it be connected to the missing manuscript? If only Fort had not been incapacitated. I would have welcomed any ideas, even the esoteric musings of the American.

Two burly Constables arrived at the office door. I made my excuses and left. There was little more I could learn, at least until I spoke to the Chief Inspector. I expected that he would be just as baffled as I was.

I hurried back to Davenport's boarding house with my now rather scruffy flowers still clutched in one hand. I should probably have gone to visit Fort and let him know about the mess at the publisher's home, but I didn't want another drunken encounter with him. It could wait until tomorrow. Cutler was not going to get any more dead.

The rain began in earnest just as I reached my street. I tried not to see it as an omen.

I hurried up the steps and knocked on Victoria's front door. She opened and I held the flowers out to her.

"For Napoleon," I said with a hopeful grin. It was not returned.

"I'm rather busy, Edward." Victoria's tone was straight from the Matterhorn: decidedly chilly.

"Oh." I dropped my arm, the flowers hanging limply by my side. "I thought you might like to go to dinner?"

"Did you."

I was never especially quick on the uptake, but I was becoming aware of something unpleasant occurring.

"Is something wrong?"

Victoria's expression was hard and unforgiving. "Not at all."

"Listen, Vic, you seem upset..."

"Do I?" I was rather horrified to see her eyes fill with tears. She sniffed and folded her arms.

"I have just been reading about your advancement in station. When you told me your father passed away, I didn't realise what you were really saying."

I was beginning to understand, and I didn't like it one little bit. "Listen, Victoria -"

"No, you listen." She disappeared for a moment, then returned, brandishing a rolled-up newspaper as if it were a sword.

"I always knew you were a posh sort... I knew you were the heir

144

to something or other. I've even met your sister. But this?" She threw down the newspaper. My foolish face jammed under a black hat stared back at me. Some press blighter had photographed me at the funeral.

"I'm sorry."

"What is there to be sorry about? You've had your fun with the common folk, now you can go back to your castle."

"It's not a castle."

"Oh?" She picked up the paper and began to read aloud. "The Duke of Bentham is expected to take residence at the ancestral home of the Fotheringham's, Highstead House in Suffolk."

"It's just the papers, Victoria. I'm not going anywhere."

"Is that true? Nothing is going to change?"

I remembered Hankey, my mother all the rest of them, and I couldn't find the words to tell her. It made no difference. Victoria read it on my face.

"Just as I thought. You've had your fun and now the game's up you'll be off to your highborn friends and forget all about the likes of us."

"I really wasn't playing at anything. I wanted…" I paused, trying to control myself. "I wanted this to be my real life. It was my real life."

"A fairytale, that's what it was. You can't just close your eyes and wish and become another person. Didn't you think about your… your friends?"

I reached out for her hand but she snatched it back.

"When were you going to tell me…" she broke off, shaking her head. "It doesn't matter. Why should I think that you owed me anything? Of course you don't." She turned away.

"Victoria, please!"

The door slammed shut. I examined the bouquet in my hand. The flowers were beginning to wilt.

Chapter 22

Fort arrived at the office the next morning half-way through the morning looking like he hadn't been to bed.

"Sorry I was a little... out of sorts yesterday, Edward," the American said, trying to smooth the wrinkles from his trousers with the palms of his hands.

"Don't mention it," I said. In truth, my meeting with Victoria had gone so badly I had little emotion left for my partner. I had a headache and was feeling generally ill at ease with the universe.

Fort gave a sad little smile and sat down at his desk.

"I went to Cutler's office yesterday," I said, once the silence had lingered for long enough. "Someone had turned it over."

Fort raised an eyebrow. "Strange order of events: murder and then robbery. One would imagine it would be more usual for them to occur the other way around."

"It's got the police stumped as well," I agreed.

"Do you think someone was searching for O'Hendry's manuscript?"

"Perhaps. And if so then was Cutler killed because he wouldn't give it up."

Fort waved a fountain pen in the air like it was a magic wand. "Which brings us back to the same problem. What could be in the manuscript worth stealing or killing for?"

"Mickey Colton is dead," a cheery voice declaimed from the office door. Fort and I looked around, our expressions of surprise mirrored on one another's faces.

Chief Inspector O'Connell let himself in and sat down heavily in the chair in front of my desk.

I felt my head spin. After my rather fruitless attempts to convince Victoria that I wasn't some sort of cad, I had retired to my room and spent the evening with a bottle of sailor's rum. It had not been a good idea.

"Are you sure?" I asked.

"There was plenty of blood but his face was still recognisable at least. His chest looked like he'd been in the ring with an African lion."

"What happened to him?" Fort asked, although he was already scribbling something on one of his little notecards. Mere murder never occupied his curiosity for long.

"Stabbed, several times. Outside his lodgings. Pockets were turned out. We might have pegged it for a robbery if you hadn't brought him to our attention. Don't suppose you have any idea who did for him?"

"No. If he wrote the letters then I suppose he may have been asking to be done in. But I'm not convinced that he did."

"Did he deny writing them when you saw him?"

I frowned. "How did you know I spoke to him?"

"We were informed that he had an altercation with a 'posh sort' and a Yank yesterday." The Chief Inspector tugged on his whiskers. "I wouldn't be much of a detective if I couldn't work that one out."

I sank down in the chair. "We went to question him about the letters."

"What did you find out?"

"Nothing. He wouldn't tell me anything, so I –" I broke off. I had just remembered about Renie. Had she managed to persuade Colton to go on a date?

"Was there any sign of anyone else hurt where you found Colton? A young woman?"

O'Connell frowned. "No, no sign of anyone, just the poor dead blighter in a pool of his own blood. You can't think a woman did this, can you?"

I shook my head. "Not at all."

"I hope you're not holding something back from me, Mr Moreton."

"Nothing that could have a bearing on his death," I said, more in hope than in truth. I should probably have told the Chief Inspector about Renie Brien, but I didn't want to get the poor girl in trouble. It had been my suggestion to get involved in Colton's life in the first place. Besides, I told myself, I had no idea if she had ever actually met the man.

O'Connell reached into his pocket. "There was one strange thing. This was found on the body."

The book was small and exquisite, like a work of art. The front cover was made from marbled paper in a rainbow of covers. Somehow I was not surprised to read the author's name. 'Kew Gardens, Virginia Woolf'. I opened it to the title page to find it had been produced by the Hogarth Press.

"Colton didn't strike me as much of a reader," Fort said as he peered over my shoulder. I turned the book over and grimaced. The delicate paper had been stained with Colton's blood.

"What is it then, some sort of message?" The Chief Inspector asked.

"If it is, I'm damned if I know what, or to whom," I grumbled.

"Literature and all that nonsense," O'Connell grunted, "just my luck. Any link to the publisher's murder?"

I shrugged. "I couldn't say."

The policeman sighed. "Well, make it your business to find out, won't you? I heard you were poking around Cutler's office yesterday."

I skirted past the hint of criticism in O'Connell's voice. "Yes. I wanted to see if there was anything we had missed. But the place had been ripped apart."

"So I heard. Got my best men searching through the mess but God knows what's meant to be there and what isn't. As if we didn't have enough to worry about. You find out any more about the letters?"

"I haven't had much of a chance."

The Chief Inspector snorted his disapproval. "I'm afraid we'll need to speak to your sister."

I felt my stomach clench. "Liz? Why?"

O'Connell straightened his collar. "Come now, Moreton, you know how it works. You told me yourself she had a history with the man."

I tried to think of some way that we could keep my sister out of it, but the man was right. She was in this up to her neck.

"Could you let me break the news to her first? She is in mourning, and I'd rather it came from me."

It was a rather cynical ploy, but O'Connell nodded agreement.

"Very well," he said, "I'll visit her tomorrow morning. I hope for your sake that she had nothing to do with this."

"I'm sure she didn't," I replied, and I just had to hope that my expression was more convincing than I felt.

Chapter 23

"My dear Edward, you know that I am perfectly capable of looking after myself," Renie Brien explained while putting a feather-topped hat back onto a shelf.

"I was worried about you," I said. "When I heard that Colton had been killed I wanted to make sure you hadn't come to any harm."

"You were afraid that you might have sent me into the lion's den, is that right?" The young American smiled. "Alas, I did not so much as get a sniff of a murderer last night."

"But you did meet Colton?"

She sighed and pulled the shutters closed. I had timed my visit so that the little boutique was closing for lunch. I had no desire to talk about a gruesome murder in front of the customers.

"Yes, I met him. I must say, I cannot feel too upset that somebody murdered him. He was a rather slimy individual."

She turned to the window display and began rearranging a collection of furs. The animals' glass eyes stared at me.

"How did you manage to find him?"

"A well-placed shilling in a dirty palm. Nothing too difficult, although I must say I heard some interesting language in the dockyards."

I gestured to her to continue.

"With the information from my little bribe I found myself at his lodgings, and from there I managed to arrange an accidental meeting with him that ended in a downmarket café. The food was truly dreadful."

"You talked him into taking you to dinner?"

"A lady should not give up all her secrets. Suffice it to say that a man of that sort does not take much convincing that a woman has taken a shine to him."

"And did you find out anything about the letters?" I interrupted. Now that I knew Renie had not been harmed, I was eager to skip ahead to the pertinent information.

She tapped a thimble against her chin. "It was not the easiest thing to just insert into the conversation. If I had asked 'have you written any threatening letters recently' it would have put rather a pallor on the dinner."

I could see her eyes glitter with excitement. "But you did get something out of him, didn't you?"

"Yes. Or, at least, I think so. At first I tried to find out about your sister. I asked him if he had any lady friends. Unfortunately he was too eager to present himself as unattached."

"I suppose even Colton would consider it ungallant to talk about a previous girlfriend at dinner with a potential replacement."

"Exactly. Then I wondered if I could compare his handwriting with your letters, so I asked him to write his address on a card."

She pulled a calling card from her purse.

"Excellent!" I exclaimed as I took the note from her hand. My excitement was short-lived, however. "What dreadful handwriting. This is nothing like the penmanship of the letters. Could he have disguised his writing somehow?"

"Perhaps," Renie said, although her expression was doubtful. "He didn't seem like letters were his forte. Anyway, I thought it

153

was time to try another tactic. I thought that he might be an accomplice to the letter writing, rather than the man himself. So I tried to engage him in helping me with a particular problem."

"How devious of you."

"We had eaten the beef. It was rather tough. Poor cooking always makes me devious. Anyway, I mentioned to Colton that I had a rather awkward situation with a competitor. Someone who wanted to put me out of business."

"You do?"

She arched one eyebrow. "Of course not. I am perfectly capable of taking care of myself. But I wondered if Colton might offer to help. Which he did immediately. There is nothing men love more than a damsel in distress."

I kept judiciously silent.

"Colton practically fell over himself to recommend a 'friend' who could make my problems disappear. I played my part well, if I do say so myself. I said that I would hate to see anyone get hurt. The man protested the point, and said that there were other ways of removing my enemies than violence."

I felt my pulse rise. "Did he mention the letters directly?"

"Not in so many words. He said that he could 'apply pressure' on my fictitious competitor. And that it could be achieved for a very reasonable price, a friend's discount, he called it," Renie said with a grimace.

"Did you get any more out of him?"

"He promised to meet me for lunch today to discuss it further."

"That will prove difficult."

"Indeed. A most annoying coincidence. If it is a coincidence?"

I nodded. "Seems unlikely. Could someone have killed Colton for being so clumsy with his information? I suppose it is possible." I banged my hand on the counter. "If only we'd been quicker!"

Renie glared. "No need to take your temper out on my store. That's real walnut, that countertop."

"Sorry."

Renie folded her arms. "I'm sorry Colton is dead."

"You weren't… seduced by the man as well?"

If looks could kill I would be lacking a pulse from the glare that the American gave me.

"Don't be an ass, Edward. He was rather harmless in his way. Like a weasel, or a ferret. Easily led astray, I should think."

I murmured noncommittedly. Colton might not be the mastermind of the letters, but I knew he had some part in them. Otherwise he would still be breathing.

"Well, I suppose I should go back to the office and tell Fort that we are no further forward. It's been a hell of a week."

I was surprised to feel Renie's hand clasp mine. "I'm sorry about your father, Edward."

"Ah, you heard about that." My mouth felt dry. "He… he had a long life. And we weren't exactly close."

"It leaves you in a difficult position, his death?"

As usual, nothing had gotten past Ms Brien.

"Nothing I can't handle," I said with false optimism.

"And the case? I suppose with Colton dead you have two murders to worry about."

"To be honest, I don't know where to start." I felt a familiar weariness overtake me. I experienced a sudden longing for Fort's brandy bottle. "Fort is being impossible. My time is running out. Corpses are appearing all over the place and I don't have the first idea of how everything is connected. I might as well give up now."

Renie stared at me for a few long seconds.

"Right," she said. "Enough of your procrastinating. It's about time you got organised."

Chapter 24

Like a small child being forced onwards by a somewhat intimidating Governess, I found myself being taken by the hand and led upstairs to the locked room where Miss Brien hid her other life.

We left the exotic fabrics and hand-made shoes behind for the more esoteric pleasures of newspaper and arcana. Not for the first time I was reminded of Fort's study, only without the smell of stale beer.

I followed Renie to her desk which was neatly stacked with reference books and stationery.

"Sit down," she ordered. I did as instructed and watched while she cleared a large area of wall space beside us. Once she had taken down all the articles and photographs that had been fixed to the wall, she turned back to face me.

"Now tell me all about the letters."

I found it easier somehow to organise my thoughts when talking to someone else. I ran through the victims of the letters and what they were being accused of. Then I listed each separate crime and the connections between them. Renie duly gave each point of interest a sheet of paper that was tacked up on the wall. Before long there was a storm cloud of paper spreading across the room.

One hour later, Renie stood back and folded her arms. She nodded in satisfaction. "There's your case, Edward. Now all you have to do is solve it."

I had to admit, I was rather impressed. I walked over to the wall and perused our creation.

First were the recipients of the letters. My sister Liz headed the list, then Bishop Gaskell and Mrs Marylebone. A thread extended from each name to a further piece of paper, elaborating the indiscretion mentioned in the letter. Next were the characters involved, suspects or otherwise. Liz's letter only produced two names: Colton and Henry Fashton. And only one of them was still living.

"I should speak to Fashton," I said.

"I would have thought that was obvious," Renie replied. "What about the other cases?"

"The Bishop and the old lady?" I had rather put them out of my mind, with all the dead bodies that had appeared recently. "Gaskell's letter accused him of wrongdoing in a trip to the Orient. I haven't found any survivors yet."

"Have you looked?"

I blushed. "I have been rather busy."

Renie sighed rather theatrically. "And the old lady?"

"Mrs Marylebone. It was her husband who was accused of wrongdoing in the letter. He's dead, so the target would be his reputation, I suppose."

"Strange to try to blackmail the dead, so long after the crime as well. No wonder this case has you flummoxed."

"Well, I wouldn't quite go that far…"

She sighed. "Would you like some help?"

I tried not to look too pathetically grateful. "Yes please."

Renie narrowed her eyes and stared at the wall. "I'll take the Bishop then. I've always found your English clergy rather endearing."

"You haven't met Gaskell. He's not the sweet and cuddly type."

"You'll manage to tackle Fashton? And then the old lady?"

"In between solving two murderers?" I said with more than a trace of bitterness. "I'm sure it will be a doddle."

Renie smiled and opened the door to allow my exit.

"You have been incredibly helpful," I said. "I don't suppose you would consider doing the same for the missing manuscript case?"

Renie's eyes narrowed. "I do have a store to run, remember?"

"Quite, quite," I said, holding up my palms in a gesture of peace. "I'll show myself out."

Chapter 25

A greyish-brown bird serenaded the morning sun outside my window. I glared at it unfavourably out of one eye. The creature's innate wholesomeness seemed to be mocking my own pitiful condition. I had knocked at Victoria's door last night several times, never receiving an answer. I told myself she was out, even though I heard a gramophone playing inside.

Best not to get distracted, I reminded myself. It wasn't as if I didn't have plenty to be getting on with. I rubbed the sleep out of my eyes and pulled on a shirt.

On my way home the previous night I had called upon Chief Inspector O'Connell to inquire about the Cutler case. The man had little to add to what I already knew. No motive had been found for the killing, nor any for the strange desecration of the offices after his death. O'Hendry still hadn't confessed, and even O'Connell was beginning to look less confident of his guilt. Unfortunately for the hapless novelist, there was no other suspect to take his place, so he seemed destined to remain at the pleasure of His Majesty for the present.

I determined that as O'Hendry was not at imminent risk of the gibbet, that I should concentrate my efforts on the case of the anonymous letters. My meeting with Renie had rejuvenated me a little. If nothing else, I did not wish to look a fool to the young American. No doubt she would produce a wealth of information on the case of Bishop Gaskell. It was up to me to do the same with the victims of the other letters.

Hence the reason for my being up with the larks, or whatever mongrel bird the creature outside my window happened to be. I wanted to get to the home of the Honourable Henry Fashton before the man had left for the day.

I dressed hurriedly and hailed a Hansom cab to take me to Belgravia. It hadn't been hard to discover the man's address: I simply looked him up in Debrett's.

The cab took me to the rather beautiful Queen Anne building that was the city home of the Fashtons. The family owned the second floor, and there was a smartly dressed concierge waiting at the door.

"Lord Fotheringham to see the Honourable Henry Fashton," I announced to the man in the velvet jacket and presented my card. I felt it was prudent to use my title. The concierge gave a nod and turned smartly on his heels.

In a few moments the man returned and beckoned me inwards. When he opened the door to the Fashton residence it was just as opulent as I had imagined.

My first thought was that I could easily see why my sister had been impressed. Every item in the apartment was the height of fashion. Chinoiserie drapes, fin de siècle black furniture... every item was brand new and selected for its appeal to the eye. Fort's entire belongings probably cost less than the brass and walnut drinks trolley.

The manservant informed me that Fashton was on his way and then he disappeared, leaving me to peer around the room without witness. I picked up a Lalique dish in which a pair of keys had been left. The genuine article. Yes, my sister, who had always loved the finer things in life, had found a fine match.

The door opened and Fashton entered, dressed for the country in his tweeds.

"I'm sorry to hear of your loss, Lord Fotheringham," the man said as he walked over, holding out a hand to shake.

161

"Thank you," I replied, letting go of the muscular grip as quickly as I could.

"You only just caught me. I am off to the estate for the weekend. A grouse hunt."

"More mindless violence," I said. Was the man really going to pretend that he hadn't recently tried to beat me to a pulp? He seemed to flinch under my glare.

"You're not here to go another round, are you?" He said with an awkward laugh.

I gave a wry smile. "Not at all. In fact, I wanted to make peace. For Liz's sake, you understand."

"How is Liz?"

I raised an eyebrow. "You would know as well as I?"

"I visited her yesterday but she wouldn't take my call."

I paused. When had I last seen Liz? Certainly not since the death of Mickey Colton. I had called her on the telephone to let her know the news, but I hadn't had a chance to visit. A pang crossed my chest. I had not been a very attentive sibling.

"She may be rather distracted," I explained. "Mickey Colton is dead."

Did Fashton look surprised at this news? It was hard to tell.

"The lad mentioned in that damned letter? Well, I can't say I'm too sorry about that. Was it drugs?"

"Drugs? Why would it be drugs?"

Fashton flinched. "I just thought... well, he was a young man wasn't he?"

I filed 'drugs' away to think about later. "He was murdered."

Fashton's cheeks reddened. "Now, now, Moreton, you don't

think I had anything to do with that?"

"Did you?"

"Listen, I mean to marry your sister. But I would not kill a man over it. Give me a little more credit than that."

I looked the man up and down. He had been quick enough to anger when he'd thought I was trying to steal his girl. Could he have stabbed Colton? Or perhaps gotten someone else to do the dirty work. If that was the case it would be the devil to prove.

"You are going to your estate today?"

"That's right. I'll be back in London on Monday."

"I might want to speak to you then," I warned.

Fashton shrugged. "Be my guest."

Chapter 26

"Mother is sleeping," Liz said when she opened the door. I shivered on the doorstep of my family's pied-a-terre on the Southern edge of Richmond Park. I was not sure if I was chilled by the wind coming from the East or the cold expression that Liz regarded me with.

"May I come in?"

"As the current owner you hardly have to ask," came the reply and I followed my sister along the tiled corridor.

Liz led the way into the drawing room. The window was open and I could hear the birds twittering away in the trees. I had driven the Ghost over in less than an hour, but it felt like a world away from bustling Belgravia.

"How is mother?" I asked.

Liz sat down on a comfortable armchair and drew her legs up beside her.

"Keeping herself busy. She seems fine one minute, then it all hits her and she just gives up. The doctor gave her some pills..."

I nodded glumly. "And how are you?"

"Do you really want to know?"

"Look Liz I'm awfully sorry I haven't been around much," I said, hating the whine in my voice. "But you know that I only irritate mother."

Liz shrugged. I wasn't sure if this cold dismissal was better or worse than being berated, which was my usual state of affairs.

"You need to speak to the lawyers," Liz said, her eyes darting to the window as if she wanted to escape through it. "There are formalities to go through. Father's estates were rather large, as you well know."

I shrugged. The longer I could put off those meetings the happier I would be.

"There is the matter of my marriage contract."

I gave a little start. "Well, I will honour whatever you arranged with father. You don't have to worry about that."

"Even if you do not approve of my future husband?"

"Liz, I have no wish to meddle in your life. I might think Fashton is a fool, but if you want to marry him then you may do as you please."

Liz tilted her head to one side. "Well, then I suppose I should be delighted by your indifference."

I fought the urge to scream. "I just want you to be free to live your life however you wish."

"We are none of us free to do that, Edward. Or have you not realised that yet?"

I decided to return to the subject of Colton's murder. It seemed rather safer ground.

"I spoke to your fiancé about Mickey Colton's death."

This brought the flush back to Liz's face. "You shouldn't have done that."

"He claimed he had nothing to do with it."

"Of course he didn't. You cannot really suspect Henry of being so... common as to knife somebody in the street?"

"A man will do terrible things in the heat of passion."

Liz laughed. "Henry is not the type."

"But if he believed you were having an affair…"

"Oh, Edward, you are a fool."

Liz put her hand to her cheek and she suddenly looked exhausted. I crouched on the floor next to her and took her hand.

"I'm sorry, Liz. I do have your best interests at heart, truly. If I do not ask these questions then Chief Inspector O'Connell will."

"All right. If you really must know… I wasn't having an affair with Colton," Liz said slowly. "He was supplying me with something."

The breath hitched in my lungs. "Drugs," I said, remembering Fashton's words.

"Yes." Liz took the silk scarf from her neck and gripped it tightly.

"What… what sort?"

She twisted her scarf around her fist. "Really… does it matter? Cocaine, the chemists call it. You needn't worry, I'm done with it all. I have been for a long time. I was never an addict."

"And Colton was your supplier?"

"I met him at a party during the war. He was handing out his little packets of powder like sweets. I never took much and I always paid on time, before you ask. I would never have let myself get into debt to a man like him."

"The letters…"

"The ones that I burned were not as discrete as the one I showed you. They mentioned the cocaine." She gave a little shiver.

"Did Fashton know?"

"Of course. I promised I had finished with the damned stuff,

166

but then I met Colton again."

"You bought more?"

"I was tired. Father was being impossible. I just needed a little something. And, of course, Colton wanted more money. I paid him a week later, but by then I had started getting the letters. It was all getting out of hand."

"You could have told me," I said.

"Could I? You were always such a moralist. I was bored, I took a little powder that alleviated the boredom, that is all. There was no harm."

"No harm for Mickey Colton?"

She turned away, but I grabbed her arm.

"Liz, please tell me honestly. Did you have anything to do with the man's death?"

She looked at me for a long time. "No, Edward. But if you ever ask me that again you can no longer consider me your sister."

The room was so quiet I could hear the grandfather clock ticking in the hall.

"I'm just trying to do my job."

"No, you're not. Your job is to be the Duke of Bentham. Right now you're just playing games."

I walked out of the room. I tried not to slam the door behind me, but it was damn tempting.

"You think Colton was killed because of drugs?" Fort asked, his feet up on his desk. It was gone five o'clock and he was still sober. I thanked heaven for small mercies.

"It is possible. That's what connects him to my sister at any

167

rate." I ran my hand through my hair, aware that I was making myself look even more dishevelled. When had I last had a decent night's sleep?

"You had no idea about the cocaine," Fort said gently.

"None at all. And bloody Fashton knows all about it. He was the one who mentioned the drugs."

"She claims she is not an addict?"

I groaned. "That's what she said."

Fort shifted in his seat. "You realise what this means for the Colton murder? And um… your sister?"

"It gives her the perfect motive. But my sister wouldn't do such a thing," I said, trying to sound more certain than I felt.

"Well then, we shall just have to prove to the Constabulary who did do it."

I gave Fort a grateful smile. "Thank you, Fort. I'm sure if we work together we can solve this case."

"I'm sorry I haven't been much help to you lately," the American said, his eyes downcast.

"Fort…" I squirmed in my chair. "I understand that you have been… unwell."

"The darkness is always waiting, Edward. Some days it is nearer than others."

"If there is anything I can do –"

"Please, let us talk of it no longer."

"Of course," I said, just as eager as my partner to move the conversation forward. "In fact, I almost forgot to tell you. I went to Cutler's place. It's been done over."

"Really? Did they damage the books?" Fort looked more

horrified than when he heard about the man's murder.

"They seemed to be looking for something. But the place was such a mess we will never know for sure if they found it or not."

"Could it be O'Hendry's manuscript?"

"Perhaps. But then why would Cutler have told us he didn't have it?"

"Teleportation," Fort said, thumping his hand upon the desk. "It could have teleported from O'Hendry's flat to the publisher's office without the man even being aware of it."

"That could be so," I said, my face carefully blank. "But it doesn't explain the break-in. Why would anyone want to rob Cutler after his death?"

Fort thought for a moment. "Perhaps it was not an item they were after. It could be a robbery as camouflage. To conceal something that our murderer would rather had stayed hidden."

"But what could that be?"

Fort opened a book and began to read. "I have no idea," he said airily. "I will leave the specifics up to you."

Chapter 27

"You had no idea that Colton was involved in drugs supply?" I asked The Sailor while we were waiting for our lamb chops to arrive.

"None whatsoever. This is rather fine port." Windmore tilted his glass so that the syrupy liquid left a coating of deep red as it moved.

I nodded. It had better be, the price I had paid for the meal. I had only managed to entice The Sailor to meet with me on the promise of a meal at the Savoy. It did not comfort me much that the now-Duke of Bentham probably didn't have to worry anymore about expenses.

The chops arrived and The Sailor attacked them with gusto. I pushed mine around the plate.

"What do the police make of Colton's death?" Windmore asked in between swallows.

"Sadly, they are as bewildered as we are."

I watched as Windmore stabbed into the pink lamb and began to feel rather queasy.

"Can't say I'm sorry he's dead," Windmore continued. "As I said before, he wasn't one of the better men I've commanded. I don't like to speak ill of the dead, mind you..."

"Anything else you can tell me about him would be helpful," I replied, filling his glass from the dark bottle on the table.

"Well, I don't suppose it matters now. He had a bunch of cronies that were just as... morally lacking as he was. They used to hang around on shore leave getting into scrapes."

"Can you remember their names?"

"There was a Jock, a MacAllister or something. And a chubby young lab from the Midlands."

"Could you let me know if you remember anyone else?"

The Sailor nodded. I took a small sip of the sickly-sweet liquid. I had hoped that Windmore might have known about the drug taking, but he didn't.

"You're sure you never saw a sign of cocaine around Colton and his gang?"

"If the men were taking these... opiates then I didn't know about it. A little too much rum was the worst we had to worry about. Chances are it had nothing to do with the navy and Colton picked up his supply somewhere else."

I wondered if Windmore was indulging in some wishful thinking. Liz had met Colton during the time he'd been enrolled in the navy. There had to be a connection between the service and the cocaine. But perhaps the Sailor was too close to the situation. I would just have to try someone else.

"Remind me to introduce you to Sir Kilsey," Windmore said suddenly.

"Who is that?"

"He's the chair of the education committee."

I gave Windmore a blank look.

"In the Lords, man!" The Sailor chuckled into his port. "I'll get him to show you the ropes. Where to go for a smoke, what to do when His Majesty himself pops in for a sherry. Don't you worry, Kilsey will see you right."

"The Lords. Of course." I could barely think over the ringing in my ears.

171

"Duke of Bentham, eh? Don't suppose you'll be doing much racing from now on."

I murmured something indistinct in reply. My stomach heaved. I watched as Windmore picked up the bone from the chop and began to chew on it. I decided to skip dessert.

Chapter 28

Food was the last thing on my mind when I returned to the office and received a telegram ordering me to meet Miss Renie Brien at the tea room at the Brown's Hotel. My stomach churned at the very notion of lunch, but I knew better than to keep the young American waiting. Thankfully Renie wanted nothing other than a light tea.

"I expect the British Government will be picking up the bill?"

"Yes," I said, "we might even stretch to a scone."

"Excellent." She beckoned a waiter over to order a cream tea. I slumped back in the comfortable chair and watched as Renie carefully placed a tiny and probably outrageously expensive hat on the seat next to her. Her gloves and coat followed, all meticulously styled for the season.

"How much does that coat sell for in your shop?" I asked.

"If you have to ask you can't afford it," she said with a laugh. "I wouldn't have thought that a Duke had to worry about such things."

"You'd be surprised what a Duke needs to worry about," I replied with a grim expression.

We waited while the waitress laid out the tea things. It would have been rude to interrupt. When the tall, fluffy scones arrived with little bowls for the cream and jam, Renie licked her lips in anticipation. I had to admit, they did smell heavenly.

"The English are infuriating in so many ways," Renie said as she smeared cream onto half a scone, "but they do know how to bake."

173

"Thank you, I think," I said. I took a small bite of scone. My delicate stomach gave a flutter and I replaced it on the plate. I was still haunted by the Sailor's bloody chops.

"Tell me about Bishop Gaskell."

Renie swallowed. "You were right, he's no mild-mannered clergyman. Quite the character, I'd say."

I nodded agreement. "He was quite happy to talk to you about the expedition?"

"I think he liked being reminded of his youth. Not the deaths of his friends, of course, he seemed genuinely upset by them. But the idea that he had once had adventures in far off lands... yes, he enjoyed telling those stories."

She licked some cream off her top lip. "But there was something odd there. I don't think it was guilt, but... it was as if he was telling the story in a certain way. Like he wanted me to see things the way he saw them. You could hardly imagine anyone ever questioning him."

"Let me guess – you did question him."

"Of course. I was really trying to find out who might want to prevent him from becoming an Archbishop."

I paused, my cup of tea halfway to my lips. "Why would anyone want to stop him becoming an Archbishop?"

Renie sighed. She opened her notepad. "You do remember the text of the letter, don't you? *I suggest you do not contest the position of Archbishop next month. Otherwise information about a certain expedition in the Orient will be made public.* It is rather an odd demand for a blackmailer, is it not?"

"I suppose is it," I said. "What did Gaskell have to say about it?"

"He muttered that there had been some opposition to his

promotion, but that it was nothing to concern him. I wasn't convinced though. He looked troubled, and I don't think he's a man who often doubts himself."

A waiter appeared to refill the teapot. Renie waited until he had disappeared once more before continuing.

"There wasn't much more to get out of Gaskell. In fact, the old man fairly clammed up once I had asked about his potential elevation. Anyway, I decided I simply had to get the recipe for the quaint little shortbread rounds the cook had made us before I left."

"Have you ever cooked a thing in your life?"

Renie grinned. "How rude you are, Edward. One might enquire after a recipe with no intention of ever cooking it. Anyway, it turned out that the cook was in need of some new stockings."

"And you just happened to have some with you?"

"It always pays to be prepared."

I poured us both a fresh cup of tea. "What did the cook have to say?"

"Gaskell is not universally liked by his parishioners. They find him rather too modern."

"Too modern? What does that mean?"

"They would prefer that he take a wife," Renie said, taking a rather unladylike gulp of tea.

"Does he have a fancy woman somewhere?"

"Not as far as I know. Or, rather, not that the cook knew about."

"Interesting."

"Not as interesting as his passion for gardening."

"Oh?"

Renie's grinned. I could tell she had discovered something good.

"In fact, he spends most of his time in the vegetable patch right at the bottom of his garden."

"Let me guess," I said, arching an eyebrow, "you were suddenly overtaken by an urge to examine the courgettes."

"The leeks actually. It turns out that the bottom of the garden backs onto a small cottage owned by one Mrs Faifley."

"Mrs Faifley? I know that name..."

"George Faifley was part of the expedition. He was one of the ones that never came home."

I thumped the table in triumph, earning myself a disapproving look from the waiter.

"Of course! Hang on a minute, Gaskell said that Faifley was a bachelor."

"And so he was. I asked Gaskell's cook about Mrs Faifley. Apparently she married young but divorced barely a year later."

"A divorcee? I would imagine the parishioners would not find her a suitable match for an Archbishop."

"Quite." The last of the scone disappeared into Renie's mouth.

I leaned forward, nearly knocking over the milk jump. "Do you think that Gaskell might have bumped off Faifley? Clear the path for himself?"

"Seems rather like over-egging the pudding, especially if the Faifley's had already divorced by this point. But Gaskell does seem rather a conscientious sort. If he thought that Faifley might expose his affair..."

I drank my tea. It had gone cold. "We'll never prove it," I said.

"No," Renie replied. "But now we know what to look for. Someone doesn't want Gaskell to be the Archbishop. There's a good chance it's connected to Faifley."

Renie reached for her hat. "Well, that is as far I managed to get. You'll have to discover the rest yourself.

"You've done ever so well," I said, and I meant it. Renie Brien was turning out to be a natural investigator. "I haven't spoken to Marylebone yet. But I did manage to corner Fashton."

A crash sounded from the direction of the kitchen. The unfortunate waiter had dropped a teapot.

"I do hope they don't take it of his wages," Renie said. "Now, tell me about Fashton."

I recounted my meeting with Fashton and my discovery of Liz and Colton's connection.

"Cocaine. I was prescribed it once for hayfever. It worked rather well as I recall. Of course, the problem comes when you want to stop taking it."

"Quite." I thought of my sister and felt the usual mix of pity and frustration. But at the edge of my mind I had the oddest feeling that I had missed something.

"Renie, why did you choose Brown's for tea?"

The American's brow furrowed. "I had heard the name recommended somewhere. Can't quite remember who told me about it. I must say, the scones were rather fine."

"You heard it in Liz's letter," I said, turning back towards the dining room. "It was where she met Colton."

Something was pushing at the corner of my mind.

"The waiter! He dropped the dish when we were talking about the letters."

The man himself emerged from the kitchen carrying a plate in each hand. He saw me looking at him, then dropped the plates and turned on his heels.

Chapter 29

"My word, Edward, you look like you could use a rest."

I had arrived back at the office red of face and somewhat dishevelled.

"I have been chasing a waiter all around Mayfair."

"What happened, did the poor man serve you an over-cooked steak?"

"Very funny," I said as I collapsed into my chair. "The man had a strange reaction when Miss Brien and I were discussing the anonymous letters. Then he ran off when I went to question him."

"Suspicious behaviour indeed," Fort said.

"Once it was clear that he had scarpered I went back to the hotel and got his home address. I'll find out what he knows in the end."

"How admirable." I could tell Fort was losing interest.

"What are you working on?"

"I'm glad you asked. I am placing myself in the centre of the maelstrom, the flux of what is and what may be."

He indicated a pile of papers on his desk.

"It certainly looks like a... ummm... flux," I said, squinting at the mess of paper in hope rather than in understanding.

"It is some files I have found that might pertain to the case of the missing manuscript."

"And Cutler's murder?"

"I am assuming that the two are connected. Now, let us examine each piece of evidence in turn. Remember the power of coincidence."

"I thought you said not to trust coincidences?"

Fort shook his head sadly. As usual, he was finding me a less than apt pupil of his method.

"Never trust science's dismissal of coincidence. The coincidences themselves, however, may provide us with enlightenment."

"Oh. That's good. What enlightenment have you found about the missing manuscript?"

"I am still of the opinion that we are looking at a case of teleportation."

"Ah," I said, all hope of an early lunch fading as Fort seemed to be positioning himself for another lecture.

"Have you ever heard of the Beast of Buchan?"

I indicated that I had not.

"Could the creature be related to the leopards that escaped a country estate in 1868? That is one theory. But what of the most obvious theory: teleportation."

"The most obvious theory?"

"An anomalous creature appears in one part of the world when it should be at home in quite another. A lynx from deepest Asia appears in the Scottish countryside. Is teleportation not the most obvious solution, whether science embraces the possibility or not?"

"And to return to the case at hand..." I prompted.

"What if O'Hendry's manuscript, like the Beast of Buchan

slipped from one geographical position to another?"

"Have you discovered any evidence in favour of this theory?"

Fort's eyes were almost wild. "Ha! I shall find it soon enough, do not worry."

There was an awkward silence. Fort slumped back down in his chair.

"But until I have discovered the manuscript, I have been keeping busy by sorting through the case notes."

"You have?"

"I have. And I have found one or two points of interest." Fort picked up a piece of paper. "Here! One such anomalous object."

"Really? Why is this so different from the rest?" It was just a piece of paper written in my own handwriting. *Miss Darlington wants O'Hendry free from prison. Why?*

Fort tapped his chin. "Do you remember when the young lady came to see us?"

"She was eager to get O'Hendry freed. Well, there's nothing unusual in that, surely? They were lovers."

"But there was something about her manner. It was inconsistent. Just consider each piece of datum. When we interviewed Darlington at her studio, she first claimed not to know O'Hendry. Next, she claimed that they had had an affair, but she was now indifferent to him. When he is arrested her demeanour changes once more. Now she is the heart-broken lover wanting to save her man. Inconsistencies of character."

"I suppose," I agree with some reluctance. It was hardly the sort of evidence that would convince Chief Inspector O'Connell to take a look at Miss Darlington. Still, it might be worth following up.   Despite his general ability to stuff more strangeness into a single sentence than any person I had ever met, Fort's theories turned out to be correct a surprising percentage of times.

"I'm going to visit old Mrs Marylebone this afternoon. I'll see Miss Darlington tomorrow and test out your theory."

"Just before you leave, there was something I had to tell you." Fort rummaged again in the overflowing paperwork and found a ripped off corner of an envelope.

"Oh yes. Hankey was in here looking for you."

I tried not to let the worry show on my face. "Was he? Did he say what it was about?"

"He said you were to go to his office as soon as possible. I assumed that he was looking for a report on what progress we have made with the Cutler case."

"I'm glad I missed him, then," I said, my shoulders sagging in relief. I tried not to think about how long it would be until Hankey blurted out my imminent departure to Fort. "We have made barely any progress at all by my reckoning."

"Ah, but what is progress? Do you mean the marching onwards of the modern scientific method? A linear fallacy, I should think.   Progress ever forwards is one of science's most pernicious myths."

"Excellent. I'll be sure to tell that to Hankey."

Chapter 30

Mrs Marylebone was unable to see visitors, as I was told sternly by the white-haired maid when I arrived just after lunch.

"Ma'am is resting," the woman said severely. Her earlier good humour seemed to have evaporated, and I got the distinct impression that I was no longer welcome. I suspected that if I even suggested waking Mrs Marylebone up I would be chased off the premises.

"I wouldn't dream of disturbing her," I said, winning a small nod from the maid. "I do however need some information. Would it be possible to speak to you somewhere convenient?"

The old woman paused for a second, then reluctantly opened the door. "I'll see you in the servant's parlour," she said. "Mind you don't keep me long."

"I won't," I replied, scurrying after her.

I was soon settled in a high-backed wooden chair that I shared with a rather elderly feline.

"Don't mind Tom," the housekeeper said as the infernal creature spiked into claws into my lap. "He's getting on a bit but he's ever so friendly." A spark of mischief in her eye told me that she knew very well the demeanour of the creature, but I determined not to disagree.

"Has your mistress received any more anonymous letters?" I asked.

"Not that I'm aware. Nasty, spiteful things. Who would send such terrible letters?"

"That's what I'm trying to find out."

The old maid passed me a teacup. I was not offered sugar.

"She took bad after you left last time," the maid said, her hand clutching a lace handkerchief. "She's only just getting over it."

"She seemed to be a strong old bird."

"They always do. Until they ain't." She blew her nose. "Still, I reckon ma'am has got a few more years left in her."

"It's Mrs Shirl, isn't it?"

"That's right."

"I have no desire to upset your mistress any further, Mrs Shirl." I leaned forward in the chair, hating myself just a little for attempting to manipulate a kindly old lady. "Perhaps you could give me the information I need, then I wouldn't have to trouble her."

The woman nodded sharply. "I'll do what I can."

"I need to know everything you can tell me about the anonymous letter."

Mrs Shirl shrugged. "I don't see what more I can tell you. I came in one morning and it had come in with the post. I only remember it because of the purple ink. I wondered if it was someone looking for money."

"Oh? And why was that?"

The woman picked up a set of teaspoons and set to polishing them with the handkerchief. "People always think that the mistress has money. Her husband left her some, that's true, but most of it is tied up in this old place. Still, she manages all right. It's not like she spends much."

"So when you saw the letter…"

"It was that funny coloured ink. I guessed it would be some

charity or other looking for a donation. I never dreamed it would be something so horrid."

"And you have no idea who might have sent it?"

"None at all."

I glowered at the cup of tea. I needed something better than this to report back to Renie, otherwise I'd be a laughing stock.

"What do you think of the contents of the letter?"

The old woman stiffened. "I think it's all a nasty lie. That's the thing about sending a letter without putting your name to it. You can be as horrid as you like and no one can question you on it. It's evil, if you ask me. Evil, pure and simple."

"Did you ever meet Reginald Platt?"

"No."

"And Mr Marylebone?"

"I knew the master for three decades before he passed away."

"Do you think that he killed Reginald Platt?"

The old woman looked at me defiantly. "He never mentioned what happened in Cornwall. And he's not here to defend himself now, is he?"

That wasn't a no, I thought to myself. "Mrs Shirl, I just want to find out who's writing these letters. What is it that you're not telling me?"

The woman rubbed her eyes. They may have been surrounded by wrinkles, but they were as sharp as ever. "I will not betray my mistress, you understand me? I've been with Mrs Marylebone since before you were born."

"I don't want to cause trouble for Mrs Marylebone. But someone else does. One man connected with these letters is

185

already dead. I am not here to waste anyone's time, least of all my own."

The old woman stood up. "Then perhaps you better go. I need to go and give the missus her medicine. She doesn't need any more upsets."

"Is she very sick?" I persisted as I was ushered towards the door.

"Her nerves are shot. She's already outlived two doctors though so I wouldn't be writing her off any time soon."

"Who will inherit the house when she dies?"

Mrs Shirl thought for a moment. "Well, she's left me a little something, I know that. You wouldn't be suggesting I'm going to poison her tea or something, would you?"

"Not at all."

"Good. And the house will go to her nephew, I suppose."

"A nephew?"

The woman smiled. "You're thinking he'll be a young cad wanting to bump her off for the money, is that right?"

"Ummn…"

"He's fifty years old and a GP in Chester."

"Right." I felt that the conversation had rather gotten away from me. I endeavoured to pull it back on track. "Listen, Mrs Shirl, I'm not looking for someone who might want to 'bump off' Mrs Marylebone. What I'm after is someone that might want to send her a threatening letter. I just can't see the motive for it."

"Well, nor can I," said Mrs Shirl, rather unhelpfully.

"And to ask for a hundred pounds. Does she have it?"

"She might have in the bank, I suppose. That's half of what has agitated her nerves. She's waiting to see if they write back to tell her what to do with the money."

"Curious that they didn't do that in the letter," I said, half to myself. "Almost as if they weren't really interested in the money at all."

"Good day," Mrs Shirl said, indicating that I should take my leave.

"You will let me know if Mrs Marylebone receives another letter?"

"I expect I shall," she said as she closed the door in my face.

"I thought little old ladies were always impressed by a man with a title." Fort was finding my lack of success with Mrs Shirl to be rather amusing.

"She was very protective of her mistress," I said, carefully writing my report of the interview. I was trying to make it seem like I had discovered lots of useful information, but the words on the page refused to obey my bidding.

"The nephew might be worth checking," Fort said. I got the feeling that he was trying to make me feel better. He never normally showed as much interest in the detail of evidence hunting.

"I suppose. How are you getting on with your teleportation research?"

"Oh, fine, just fine," Fort said in the manner of one who had forgotten all about it.

"I thought I might show Mrs Woolf some of the letters," I said to Fort. "If someone she knew stole the ink, then she might just recognise the handwriting."

"Good idea," Fort replied. "She has the eye of a poet, and what is poetry but the expression of observation? Go and ask Mrs Woolf your question, my friend, that woman is a keen observer."

I felt rather proud that Fort approved of my thinking for once.

"There is something troubling me about these letters," Fort said, watching me through his spectacles. "I am worried about the hundred pounds demanded from Mrs Marylebone. Why would they ask for money, commit this blackmail without directing the woman how to pay them?"

"I know. It's the same with Bishop Gaskell's letter. Blackmailing someone to stop them being promoted in the Anglican church. It just all seems a little ridiculous."

Fort banged his fist on the desk. "The letters have no consistency. Neither one thing nor the other. If I were to write such things they would be much more cutting."

"Would they?" I said, momentarily derailed by the sort of threatening letters a phenomenologist might write.

"They would be vitriolic like you have never before experienced in your life. People would be falling over themselves to pay me money. Be thankful that I have chosen the path of righteousness, Edward." Fort paused, then held up Liz's letter. "But these specimens that we have been asked to examine. They have been put together from hints and poor grammar and cliché. There is an air of madness to them and I do not like it one bit."

I found myself nodding. Nothing about the case quite made sense. Of course, I was used to feeling baffled. After all, I had Charles Fort for a partner. But rarely had I been so at a loss to know where to begin.

Fort leaned back in his chair. "And yet… some elements seem calculated. Colton's death. That was no accident. There must be some reason behind it."

There was a knock at the door and Chief Inspector O'Connell entered, shaking the rain from his greatcoat.

"Cats and dogs out there," he said. Fort reached over to protect his papers from the moisture.

"We've had to let O'Hendry go," the Chief Inspector said with an air of mournfulness.

"I thought you had him pegged for Cutler's death?"

"Still do. But for the moment the Darlington girl is giving him an alibi for the murder. I think she's covering for him, but there's not much I can do for the moment. I'll speak to the judge first thing tomorrow and try and convince him to go to court. That's if the slimy character doesn't do a runner before then."

"I still don't think he did it. Cutler was going to publish his book. Why would he kill him?"

"These artistic types don't need a reason. One minute they're as sane as you or I, the next they flip."

There was a pause during which time the Chief Inspector and myself did our best not to look at Fort.

"There were any number of artistic types involved with Cutler, so if you're going down that road it might be worth interviewing some of the others."

The Chief Inspector raised an eyebrow. "We did interview one or two. That Mrs Woolf is a little… unstable, is she not?"

My eyebrows arched. "You cannot possibly think…"

"That she murdered Cutler? Perhaps not. But what about the poison pen letters?"

"You think that Virginia Woolf could be the letter writer?"

The Chief shrugged. "Is it beyond the realms of possibility? You told me yourself that she owned the purple ink. The woman has had a series of breakdowns, I believe."

I could not explain why I felt that Mrs Woolf could not have written the letters. "I don't see it. She is not malicious," I said, with the sense that it was a rather lame excuse.

The Chief Inspector pulled on his coat. "Just because you feel sorry for her does not mean that she is not the culprit. If you do not come up with someone more likely then I shall bring her in for questioning. Authors. Barmy, the lot of them."

There was a frosty silence from Fort's side of the desk.

"Present company excluded, of course," O'Connell said quickly, then closed the door behind him.

Chapter 31

I spent my lunch hour searching for Victoria. I wouldn't have admitted that was what I was doing, of course. I told Fort I was merely going out to stretch my legs.

There was no sign of her, although I did earn myself some sniggers as I walked past the typing pool. No doubt about it, she was avoiding me.

Perhaps it was for the best. The lovely Miss MacMillan would only have asked me what I was going to do about my hereditary problems – pun intended – and I had no answer for that. My sister would have called it denial. I merely thought of it as survival.

At one point I saw Hankey emerge from a meeting room. I only just had enough time to flatten myself against a stairwell before the man walked past. I stayed there, lost in the shadows until there was no one else in the corridor.

By now I was feeling truly sorry for myself. I should probably just accept my fate. Take up my position in the Lords. Move to my country estate. Live the life of the landed gentry. God knows there would be people that would kill for that sort of life. And yet...

"Moreton!" Fort bellowed down the corridor. I flinched at his voice, then did a double take when I took in his appearance. The American was always somewhat shabbily dressed, but his clothes looked like he had slept in them. Perhaps he had. I could almost smell the brandy from the other end of the corridor.

"I seem to have lost our office!"

How on earth had he got in such a state since this morning? I took him gently by the arm.

"Don't worry old chap," I said, trying to show some sympathy when a large part of me just wanted to give him a smack on the chops. "I'll show you the way."

By some miracle of God or whatever strange deities Charles Fort might have worshipped, we made it back to our little office without any of our superiors spotting us.

"Let me get you some coffee," I said and poured some lukewarm brown liquid from the pot I had hastily liberated from the secretary's office.

"Thank you," Fort replied, his early bluster disappearing. I watched him sip the coffee. Fort looked dreadful. His eyes were grey and sunken in his face and his hands were trembling.

"Fort..." I paused, not sure how to approach the subject. "You don't think you've been overdoing it, do you?"

He stared up at me with a baleful expression. We both knew what I meant by 'it'. Brandy, beer... whatever was available and came from a glass.

"I only meant to have a quick drink with lunch," he said, his head hung in shame. "It is this damned case."

"The death of Cutler?"

"The publisher's death is only a small part of it. The anomalous items that proceed together to become a flood." Fort half-closed his eyes. "I have always considered myself a writer, above everything else. But this week has taught me that writers are little more than flotsam, destined to float on the seething sea of public opinion. I read one of Simmonds novels. Do you remember, we met him in the bar?"

The conversation was not going in the direction I had been expecting. "Yes," I answered, "but I did not think he would be the sort of author that would appeal to you."

"I spotted the book in a second-hand shop. Paid a ha'penny for it. It was a dreadful thing. Set during the war, a tale of daring-do with men shooting each other and making love to women and barely a word longer than two syllables. And it's made him a fortune."

"But Fort, you cannot envy the man. You are writing something very different."

"I am not writing what the public want. Oh, I do not want to make my fortune, nothing as base as that. But to be read, for enough people to hold my work in their hands and think: Yes, this has worth. That would be enough. Yet even at this I have failed."

"And this is what has sent you into this… funk?"

"I do not expect you to understand, Edward."

Lord save me from the artistic temperament, I thought. I found myself grateful – not for the first time – that I was untroubled by Fort's level of intellect. I was reminded of Mrs Woolf's sad eyes. There was something to be said for avoiding the spark of genius. It did not seem to make one very happy.

"I'm sure that the Bloomsbury set could never stop a vampire,"

I said to Fort, forcing my voice to sound jolly. "Or a poisoner, or a murderer of old ladies."

"That is true. But long after we are gone, it is the words that will endure, not our actions. For prosperity it is not existence that matters, but utterance."

"Mmn," I said, being careful to neither agree nor disagree. After all, I hadn't the faintest idea what he was talking about.

"Oh, I came across this picture in my research. I was looking for instances of the Bloomsburys in the papers. Apparently, this one made rather a stir at the time." Fort rummaged around in one of the huge piles of paper that littered his desk until his hand clenched around a single sheet.

It was a picture of a group of people in exotic costumes. Their faces were dark with thick black beards. They looked more than a little odd, something that was soon explained by the article.

"*The Abyssinian Hoax,*" I read. "*The Royal Navy was outfoxed yesterday by a group of men dressed as members of an African royal visit. In fact, these individuals were perpetrating an artful hoax. They were Englishmen – and one woman – wearing an exotic disguise. Questions are to be asked before parliament as to how these people made their way on board one of His Majesty's most important ships.* Good Lord, Fort, Virginia Woolf was one of the men! Or woman, rather."

"How strange," Fort said. "What were they trying to achieve?"

"To make fools of the Navy? The article doesn't say."

Fort tapped the article with his finger. "An anomalous event.

You can be sure that this is relevant to our investigation."

"All right," I said, but I was not convinced. The article was from ten years ago. I couldn't see how it was relevant to the case at hand. But I trusted Fort's instinct. He wasn't always right, but he was always interesting.

"I think I will ask Mrs Woolf about this."

"Good idea," Fort replied, already lost in his research. At least the coffee seemed to have done its work. He was so engrossed that he didn't even notice when I left the office.

"The Abyssinian hoax." A small smile played around Virginia Woolf's lips. "That was a long time ago. How extraordinary to think I was ever that young."

I sipped on some sort of herbal tea that Leonard Woolf had made for me. Mrs Woolf had seemed glad of the interruption when I had knocked upon her door.

"How pleasant to think of earlier times," she said as she peered at the photograph I had handed her. "The writing is not going well today."

In that short phrase I felt that I could understand everything about her mood. I turned to her husband.

"Were you involved in the hoax?"

Leonard Woolf looked a little uncomfortable. "Before my time."

"Yes, a more innocent age." A little colour had come into Mrs Woolf's cheeks. "My cousin and I... Well, there was this ruse, you see, that we would go aboard a ship in oriental disguise.

Pretend to be visiting Sultans, that sort of thing."

"They believed you were a Sultan?" I asked, incredulous.

"We played our parts rather well, I like to think. We had the men fooled all right. They were mocked rather badly in the press for it."

"And was that the end of the matter?"

"Of course."

"There was nothing more to it?"

Mrs Woolf stared at me with those mournful eyes.

"Leonard," she said, "could you bring Mr Moreton a small coffee? He looks like he might need something to revive him."

"That would be very kind, thank you."

The man hesitated for a moment, but his wife just smiled sweetly at him. With a last puzzled glance, he hurried downstairs.

When he left, Mrs Woolf walked over to her desk and began to shuffle through a pile of papers. I waited patiently, unsure of what was happening but unwilling to do anything that might break the spell.

"Here we are," Mrs Woolf pressed a newspaper cutting into my hand. It was a little creased, but I knew I was looking at a photograph of the perpetrators of the hoax. Unlike in the newspaper they were sitting down, relaxing even. I wondered how the Naval men had ever failed to spot that one of their Sultan's was clearly female.

Mrs Woolf had moved over to the window, her eyes following the people rushing by on the street below.

"Was there something you wanted to tell me about the hoax?" I asked.

The author leaned against the windowsill, as if the wood was supporting her weight, though she seemed to be lighter than a feather there was so little to her.

"Do you have children, Mr Moreton?"

"No," I replied, slightly thrown by the change in subject.

"To bring another being into this world... It is almost unimaginable, is it not? What they might become when one's back is turned."

I kept silent, wondering where the woman was going.

"I have thought for a long time that my works are like my children. It is overly simplistic, of course. And yet... there is something appealing about the idea. They resemble me in so many ways, yet they are so different."

I coughed politely. I had found the tactic worked to shake Fort out of similar moods.

"Ah yes. You want to know about the Dreadnought. I was just thinking that our actions might be considered the children of our thoughts. And what do my actions on the ship that day tell you about me?"

I was starting to sweat. I found myself longing to interrogate Mickey Colton again. At least the worst he could give me was a beating. Speaking to Mrs Woolf felt like my head was being put through a mangle.

"That you enjoy a prank," I said slowly. "And that you do not take yourself too seriously?"

I was rewarded with that transformational smile once more. "Oh, I hope that you do see that. I do not take myself seriously at all - indeed, how could I with all my little failures and triumphs. But the work… now that I take more seriously than anything on earth."

I searched around for a lifebelt.

"Did you ever find out who stole your purple ink?"

The smile vanished. "No," she said softly, but I noticed her right hand had bunched into a fist. Virginia Woolf knew more than she was letting on.

"I'll see myself out," I said and she nodded absently. Just as I turned to go I remembered something. "There was something else I wanted to ask you. We spoke to Mr Simmonds. He made a … well, I suppose you could call it an allegation. There was an article in The Strand about his work. A rather unflattering one. He suggested that you might have written it."

Mrs Woolf smiled her sad smile. "Simmonds rather overestimates my interest in his work, I'm afraid. No, I did not write a single word about the man. Leonard showed me the review. It was rather harsh."

"Simmonds suggested that it had put your husband off publishing his latest book."

"We wouldn't have published it anyway. We have enough work to keep us busy. Too much, in fact. And I have my own work…"

She drifted off into silence.

"Could Strachey have written the article?"

Her eyes focused back on mine. "Lytton is not often backward in claiming his own opinions. It is more likely to be some minor author out to make mischief."

"Someone fond of a prank?"

Now the smile reappeared. "My pranking days are over, Mr Moreton."

Chapter 32

An hour later I returned to the office, only to see the large figure of Chief Inspector O'Connell sitting in my office chair. There was no sign of Fort and I thought he'd probably snuck home to get an early night.

"I've been looking for you," O'Connell said.

"Not more murders I hope," I said lightly.

The policeman coughed. I stared down at him.

"It isn't another one, is it?"

"It is Miss Darlington."

"Not... not dead?" I grimaced. The people involved in this case were dropping like flies.

"No, not yet at any rate. She's in the infirmary. Took a nasty knock to the head. It was one of our lot that found her. The Constable was going to interview her about O'Hendry. She was going to be a character witness, make a statement saying what a decent bloke he was." Chief O'Connell sniffed to indicate he thought this unlikely.

"You can't think O'Hendry hurt her?"

"Seems unlikely. Miss Darlington was doing her best to get him off Cutler's murder. The man's a blackguard, but I can't see him being foolish enough to bite the hand that feeds him. No, we're looking for someone else. The woman was knocked half-senseless, she claims can't remember a thing about the man who did it."

I groaned. Why on earth had the young artist been targeted? This was simply the most infuriating case.

"I wanted to tell Mr Fort, but I haven't found him."

"He's doing practical experiments again," I explained. I did not mention that Fort had not been managing to keep to his sobriety vow. O'Connell was not a man who had much sympathy for the artistic temperament, especially the kind that was only soothed by the bottle.

"Ah." The Chief Inspector looked at his pocket watch. "I can't wait, I'm afraid. If Miss Darlington makes it through the night we'll try and interview her tomorrow. I don't suppose you have any idea who is going around bumping off all these people?"

"I'm working on it," I said.

"I should work a little faster if I were you. Word is you might not be around here much longer."

"Who told you that?"

O'Connell shrugged. "Common knowledge. You got the big promotion I guess."

"A promotion? It doesn't feel like that."

The Chief Inspector pulled on his whiskers. "There's folk that would kill for the easy life, you know? Turn up in the Lords and vote once a month, shooting estates for the summer. Sounds like a grand old time to me."

I folded my arms. "I suppose it will be."

The Chief Inspector turned to leave. "Still, I have to admit I'm a little disappointed. I thought there was a little bit more about you than that."

I bit my lip, not trusting myself to speak.

I found O'Hendry not an hour later, sitting in a fashionable cocktail bar in Fitzrovia surrounded by young women.

He was sitting on a chaise, his chin propped up by his hand. With his other hand he gestured toward the window.

"Ah, that little tent of blue we prisoners called the sky, and at every careless cloud that passed in happy freedom by," he said.

"Beautiful," one of the women murmured.

"Oscar Wilde, isn't it?" I said, standing over them.

The author's face darkened. "Of course. I was merely paying tribute to the great Irishman. Would you ladies leave us? I need to have a word with my colleague here."

The ladies left to find another table. I sat down next to O'Hendry.

"I suppose I owe you a thank you," the man said with bad grace. "The old fool of a Chief Inspector told me you thought I was innocent."

"O'Connell is no fool. The evidence against you did look rather damning. But there was no motive."

"Of course there wasn't. I'd hardly kill the old man when he was about to publish Delphinium, would I?"

"I don't suppose your manuscript has turned up?"

O'Hendry took a gulp of beer. "No it bloody well hasn't. Weren't you lot meant to be looking for it?"

"We have been rather busy."

"With what?"

"The brutal murder of the publisher," I said, somewhat tetchily.

"Damn Cutler and his enterprise," O'Hendry said, flecks of spittle spraying from his mouth. "The man brought me nothing but trouble. None of this would have happened if you had found my manuscript."

What a small-minded, obnoxious man, I thought. It was rather a shame I had saved him from the gallows.

"Did you hear that Eliza Darlington has been attacked."

The Rake nodded. "It's that studio of hers. They don't lock the doors. Any ruffian could walk in."

"You didn't have anything to do with her injuries?"

"Hardly. Why would I want to hurt Eliza? She may paint dreadfully but she is terribly handy to have around."

Like if you need an alibi for a murder, I thought, though I kept my mouth shut. Now that O'Connell had decided that O'Hendry was no longer a likely murderer, I found myself trusting the man even less than before.

"I happen to know that someone else was rather fond of Eliza," O'Hendry said airily, his eyes focussed on the group of young women who were now sipping glasses of sherry.

"Oh? Who was that?"

"Simmonds. The writer of the masses. I saw him chasing after her the other day."

"Chasing after her?"

"Yes. I assumed at the time that he wanted to take her back to his apartment, if you understand my meaning." O'Hendry looked thoughtful. "Although now you come to mention it, he might have been arguing with her. Love and hate look pretty alike after midnight, don't you think?"

Chapter 33

I collected Fort at the office and hailed a cab to take us to Simmonds private rooms near the river.

"You are always rushing off somewhere," Fort argued as the cab raced past Westminster.

"Be glad that the Rolls is being serviced," I said to my American friend. "It can certainly outpace these old Unics. Half of them were being blown up during the war."

"Mmn," Fort kept his eyes out of the window. He showed the same interest when I talked about motorcars as I did when he mentioned rains of fish.

"Popular fiction must pay rather well," Fort grumbled when we arrived at Simmond's home. It was the lower conversion of a very attractive Victorian red brick building. We rapped on the door.

The author himself answered, and Fort and I simultaneously took a step backward. Simmonds was wearing a rather startling red silk housecoat of the kimono style. Thankfully he was wearing his shirt and trousers underneath.

"I was writing," he growled when he saw who had called.

"We won't keep you long," Fort said. "But if we could just ask a couple of questions?"

Simmonds shrugged and opened the door just wide enough to let us in. He led us into a living room that would have been attractive were it not for the smell of stale cigarettes and burnt toast.

"Sorry about the clothes," Simmonds said, although his smirk suggested he was amused by my obvious discomfort. "I like to be comfortable when I write. You are just lucky that you didn't find me in the bath."

I tried to ignore the unwelcome image that that suggested.

"Did you know that Eliza Darlington was attacked. She's in hospital with a damaged skull."

"I heard just this morning. Poor girl. We are none of us safe in our beds. Just the sort of thing we fought a war to stop."

I wasn't sure this entirely made sense, but I wasn't here to quibble with the author. I wanted information.

"What were you arguing with Darlington about before she was attacked?" I asked, dispensing with small talk.

"We weren't arguing."

I looked at Fort and rolled my eyes. Why did they never make it easy for us?

"You were seen chasing after her sometime after midnight."

Simmonds chewed the inside of his cheek, then seemed to come to a decision. "All right. Yes, I argued with the girl. I found out that she was Mr Bloom S Bury."

It took me a moment to work out, but Fort was quicker on the uptake.

"The article that criticised your work? It was Eliza Darlington who wrote it?"

"That's right. The little ingrate was happy enough to come to my parties and drink my wine, then she had the nerve to slander me behind my back."

I stood up. "I think it would be for the best if you came to speak to the Chief Inspector."

"Why?" The man looked genuinely shocked.

"Eliza Darlington wrote the scathing review of your latest book. The article that stopped Cutler from publishing you. And now that same lady is in the hospital."

"Now, really!" Simmonds choked back a laugh. "You cannot think that –"

Fort took up the theme. "You visited Cutler just before he died. You argued with him."

"I argue with a good many people you impudent oik! Many of them on a daily basis. That does not mean that I am in the habit of murdering them!"

The man's face was becoming the colour of his dressing gown.

"I think you should calm down, Mr Simmonds."

"That's it!" The man swung in a wild punch. I grabbed his arm and he collapsed onto the floor.

"You are being a damned fool," I hissed.

Simmonds looked up at me. "If I was in my prime I would have thrown you across the room. May I sit up."

The man seemed to have calmed down a little, so I let him climb back into his chair. He took out a dirty handkerchief and mopped at his brow.

"All right. Now why don't you take a look at this and I'll tell you just why I couldn't have murdered anyone." I don't know what I was expecting, but I was surprised when the man held out his right hand.

"You do realise your hand is empty, don't you?" Fort said after a moment of silence.

"Just watch," Simmonds said sharply. After another ten

seconds, the hand began to shake. Tremors started in the fingers and worked their way upwards until half of his upper body was shaking.

Simmonds dropped the hand to his side. "You see, Mr Fort, that's why I couldn't land a punch on your young friend here. And it's why I couldn't have bashed anyone's brains out. They call it shell shock, but they use those words for any wartime injury. Its nerve damage in my shoulder. Had a bad fall off a horse in '17."

I rubbed a hand over my chin. He could be faking it, of course. But I could see from his face how difficult it had been to admit to any weakness.

I was just about to tell Fort to leave when I realised that there was a stain on my wrist. It was ink. Purple ink.

"Fort..." I held up my arm. The American's eyes widened. We both turned back to Simmonds.

The novelist caught the look in my eye. "What is it now?"

"Let me see that hand again."

The man held out his palm. Sure enough, his thumb and forefinger were stained with ink.

"Are you fond of writing letters?" I asked.

The large man's brow furrowed. "Not any more fond than anyone else. What the devil is this about?"

"You'll have heard that we are investigating a series of anonymous letters? Some members of the Bloomsbury set have been set them."

"I told you, I have little enough to do with the infernal Bloomsburys."

"You did mention that," I continued, getting into my stride. "In fact, you told us how much you disliked them. It occurs to me that you might have everything to gain by writing anonymous letters."

"You think I am this poison pen writer? Don't make me laugh."

"I fail to see anything funny about the situation," I said sternly.

"Well then, you need to examine your sense of humour. The idea that I would write the letters is preposterous. Not least because I have received several myself."

The silence filled the room.

"You have received one of the letters?" I said when I located my tongue.

"Several, in fact."

"What did they say?"

Simmonds grimaced. "They accused me of falsifying my war record. Of trading off the heroism of others. They were nasty little things and I had no hesitancy in burning them."

"So you have no proof that you actually received any?"

"No. But unless you and Mr Fort are going to arrest me then I do not believe I need any proof."

"And what of the ink stain on your hand. The letters were written in a particular shade of purple ink."

"Purple? Come now, this is the finest red ink from Japan." I looked at my hand once more. Was it a little less purple than I had imagined at first glance? Now that I looked more closely, it did seem to have a reddish tinge.

Thirty seconds later, Fort and I were shown the door.

"Well, that could have gone better," I said.

We had scurried out of Simmonds's apartment with the man

208

bawling insults after us.

"A writer of war stories for boys that never grew up. No wonder he cannot keep his temper."

"Perhaps he does not like being falsely accused. I really thought we were getting somewhere."

"Worry not, Edward. We'll crack this case in the end."

I felt a drop of rain land upon my brow. I did not share my partner's optimism.

Chapter 34

Fort and I ended up in the lounge bar of a dark little public house just around the corner from our office. Our drinks sat in front of us, untouched. We were both more than a little shaken by our failure with Simmonds.

"He still might be Cutler's killer," I said, although my heart was not really in it.

"It would have been a wonderful coincidence if he'd turned out to be both murderer and letter writer. Alas, I fear he has proven to be neither." Fort polished his spectacles, although how he could see any dirt in the dim light of the bar was beyond me.

"Why do your coincidences never seem to work in our favour?" I said glumly.

"It is not the way of the world to bend itself to the observationalist, much as we might wish it were so. It is only our job to find the fine threads holding the spider's web of anomalous occurrences together.

"Here's another of your anomalous occurrences. Why did Colton die with this in his pocket?" I fished out the copy of 'Kew Gardens' that I had been carrying around in my waistcoat pocket.

"Perhaps a present for a young lady?"

"That could be, I suppose. I wonder where he got it from. I shall ask Mrs Woolf where her books are sold."

Fort seemed to be sketching some sort of beetle in his notebook. "In a bookstore, I would imagine."

"Thank you very much." I looked out of the tiny office to see rain dribbling down the glass. "Could the Woolfs have been involved in Colton's murder somehow?"

"It is unlikely. But then, likelihood is not the best judge of action, am I right? One must consider the datum independently and then severally."

"All right." I wondered if the rain would stop before I had to go outside.

"Are you listening, Edward?"

"Of course," I said, startled.

"Go back to the Woolfs. Bloomsbury is right at the heart of this mess. I am sure of it."

"You say that you found this in a dead man's pocket? How macabre."

Virginia Woolf was sitting at her desk in the window. The sun streamed in but it didn't seem to bring much warmth with it. I shivered despite my woollen suit.

When I had arrived back at their home once more, Leonard Woolf had simply led me upstairs without a word. I suspected that the patience of the man was wearing thin. But Fort's words rang in my ears. Bloomsbury was at the heart of everything. I just had to work out how.

"Did you print many of them?"

She turned the book over in her hands. "No. A limited edition in fact. And you say that the dead man would not have been much of a reader?"

"Not from what I heard."

"Well, one never knows who might be touched by a stray thought from another human being."

"Where did you sell the books?"

"Most people found us. Literary connoisseurs. A few bookshops stock Hogarth press works."

"So there is no way of telling who this belonged to?"

"I'm afraid not."

Another dead end, I thought. But while I was there I couldn't help but ask about something that had been on my mind.

"You're sure that there wasn't something you wanted to tell me about the Dreadnought?"

She snapped her head around and gave me an irritated look. "Not this again. I have already told you all about it. There really is nothing else to tell."

"Then why do you look so anxious?"

She laughed. "Because it is my usual demeanour."

"And the hoax was just that. A hoax."

"It was a little joke. At the expense of the pompous authorities." Mrs Woolf stared out of the window. If it was just a joke, then why did she refuse to meet my eye?

She shivered slightly as a chill draft passed through the air.

"Anything you tell me will be in the strictest confidence," I said softly. "You can count on that."

She still kept her eyes on the street below and said nothing. I tried another approach.

"It seems to me," I said, "that someone with your intellect would not be interested in a simple hoax."

Now she met my eyes, her expression bright. "You seek to flatter my ego? Come now, you are better than that."

I folded my arms. "I may not be as clever as you, Mrs Woolf, but I am determined. I want to know what you were doing on board the Dreadnought. It may concern the murders of innocent people."

She turned again to the window, watching the people outside scurrying along the pavement.

"I have always felt… different, Mr Moreton. Not through my writing, although some have said that it sets me apart from my peers. No, I have always felt somewhat… apart from everyone around me. An observer, rather than a participant in life. At times I have felt like I am acting my part. One day, a long time ago, a young civil servant not unlike yourself asked my friends and I if we would like to act in a play. A play that would allow us to access a ship and retrieve some sensitive documents that might have fallen into the wrong hands. We were told it might prevent a war."

Mrs Woolf's hand trembled as she reached out to touch the glass, her finger tracing patterns on the surface.

"The war came anyway, as I'm sure you are aware. All was for nothing."

I thought for a moment. "The nature of the documents?"

Mrs Woolf gave me a knowing look. "I will not expose that, even now. Indeed, we were not told at the time, although I had my suspicions."

"But someone has tried to get it out of you, haven't they? Perhaps they have sent you a letter?"

That radiant smile appeared once more. "Well done, Mr Moreton. I wasn't sure if you had worked it out."

213

I found my brain was furiously trying to catch up with my mouth. "You received an anonymous letter that threatened to expose the true meaning of the Dreadnought hoax."

"Just so. It was completely out of the blue. Three, no, maybe four weeks ago. It gave me quite a turn."

"I don't suppose you still have it?"

"I showed it to Leonard and he burned it. Now, don't be upset at him. He saw that it had upset me and he wanted to protect me. He is very kind like that."

I realised I had missed something important. "Hold on, you received the letter last month?"

"That's right."

I rubbed my eyes. "Then I have been going about this all wrong. Yours was the first letter."

"Was it? Perhaps I should feel special." She shivered. "It is a cliché of course, but they are dreadfully cowardly things. An anonymous letter. To write without disclosing yourself..."

"What do you think of the writer? I would be interested to hear your point of view."

"I should think it is someone in denial of themselves. It is a work of pretence. You see the inconsistent phrasing, the deliberate attempt to appear uneducated. And to insinuate such things about other people... But if you do not tell the truth about other people, you cannot tell it about yourself."

I frowned. I had just about followed her, but I still felt like I was running behind the woman, trying desperately to catch up. "You think the letters are deliberately constructed to present the writer as uneducated?"

"Just so. There is artfulness here, of a sort."

I felt like I was getting a little closer to... something. But it was still just out of reach.

"Did you ever have any more ideas about who might have stolen the purple ink? It is the same as was used for the letters, is it not?"

Mrs Woolf frowned. "I didn't make the connection at the time, but I suppose it might be the same ink. But that means..." She shook her head as if clearing an unpleasant thought.

"Is there anything you want to tell me?"

"No."

"Please, Mrs Woolf, the ink... People have been murdered."

Woolf sighed. "It was the young girl. I felt sorry for her. I have always believed that it is harder for women to write than men. No, not harder. An almost impossibility. For an author of my own sex to create something that stands both beside and against that canon of male literature... I felt I should be more kind, perhaps, to a woman trying to be an artist."

"It was Miss Darlington," I said, finally understanding. "She took the ink."

"I had invited her to my house. And she stole from me. I could just about forgive the poor girl for that. Such a shame her paintings are so terrible."

Chapter 35

"So near, Fort! I was so near!" I wailed as the American calmly arranged his collection of prehistoric flints.

"Hush now my young friend. Chief Inspector O'Connell says that they will interview Miss Darlington just as soon as she regains consciousness."

It was just my luck that I had managed to find a promising suspect in the case of the anonymous letters at the very moment that she had become comatose.

I laid my head on the desk. It was cool and comforting. Perhaps if I closed my eyes the rest of the world might just disappear. What a lovely thought.

"Did I ever tell you the story of the epidemic of Boulley?"

"Not now, Fort," I muttered, not raising my head.

"It was just after the Franco-Prussian war. A series of anomalous events occurred, one of which was the appearance of strange symbols on the windowpanes of the town. Religious symbols, in the main, crucifixes and so-forth. A detail of Prussian soldiers was sent to one house in particular that was reported to have an image of a band of French infantry and their flags. The pictures, it was reported only came out in the daylight. The soldiers cared little for this and destroyed the windows anyway."

In spite of myself I lifted my head from the table to glare at Fort. "And just what exactly was the purpose of that anecdote?"

"To take you out of your ill humour?"

It had distracted me for a moment. Now I was merely irritated rather than depressed.

"Nothing else?" I said, sitting up and rubbing my face.

"To point to the foolishness of our fellow men? How quick we are to rush in and how to slow to consider our actions. Thought must preface action at all point if we are to follow the phenomenologists' methodology."

I placed my hands on the desk and pushed myself upright. "All right, Fort, I won't sulk any longer."

"We are making progress, although you may not feel that way. See how far you have come with your investigations into the anonymous letters. Even without being able to interview Darlington, you have almost solved the case."

"I wouldn't go that far. We might have an idea who wrote the letters, but I still do not understand why. What was Darlington's connection to the Bishop and Mrs Marylebone? Or to my sister, for that matter?"

"Telegram!" A boy shouted from the doorway. "Telegram for Edward Moreton."

"Over here," I took the yellow envelope from his hand and the young lad disappeared.

"It's from Renie," I said as I scanned the contents.

Meeting Mrs Faifley in 1 hour STOP Potter's tea room just off Bank street STOP don't bring Fort END

"I better hurry," I said, pulling on my overcoat. "She's meeting Gaskell's fancy woman."

"Do you want me to accompany you?"

"Better if you stay in the office," I said quickly. "Just in case O'Connell wants to speak to us."

217

"I hope there are no interruptions, even from our friend the policeman," Fort said. "Neolithic arrowheads wait for no man."

Mrs Faifley was not what I had been expecting. I had imagined that the secret lover of a Bishop might be glamorous, a woman of mystery. I had not expected a rather frumpy lady of late middle age.

Mrs Renie poured the woman a cup of tea.

"I was so interested to hear that you had been fundraising for the Madagascan tortoise fund and welfare centre. It is just the sort of thing that Mr Moreton would be interested in."

Renie had explained to me that I was to play the wealthy philanthropist.

"Rich but dim," she hissed as we entered the tearoom. "I'm sure you'll manage to act the part."

Mrs Faifley fussed with her hair. "The Madagascan turtle rescue and birth centre. It is a terribly worthy cause. Those poor little creatures have a terrible time of it."

Over the next half an hour I learned more about turtles and the habits thereof than I had ever desired to know. I got the impression that Fort would have been fascinated by the woman's ability to describe every minute detail of the tiresome creatures. Perhaps that was why Renie had warned me not to bring him.

Just as I was beginning to doze off, Renie nudged my arm.

"I hear you have a rather illustrious neighbour," I said when there was a second's pause in the monologue. "Tipped to be the next Archbishop, isn't he?"

"You mean Bishop Gaskell? There has been some talk of him

moving to the position in the Cathedral. Fifty miles away! But I'm afraid I hardly know him." If I hadn't been looking for it I wouldn't have noticed the change in her expression. It was like Mrs Faifley closed down all emotion.

"There has been some opposition to his appointment, I believe."

"Is that right?" Mrs Faifley drank her tea.

"Mr Moreton contributes to several charities, don't you?" Renie said, clearly eager to get the woman back on side.

"That's right," I said, trying to play my part. "One does what one can."

"We've just returned from a benefit for the Widows and Orphans fund," Renie said, leaving a pregnant cause.

"I was widowed myself," Mrs Faifley said, filling the silence. I could almost feel Renie's glee beside me.

"I'm so sorry. Was it during the war?"

"Before that. We were actually... we were living apart. But I still loved him."

Mrs Faifley's eyes drifted over to the window. She was lost in remembrance now.

"What happened?" I asked softly, trying not to break the spell.

"He died abroad. I never quite got over it."

"One never does," Renie replied.

"If I were to love another man," Mrs Faifley blushed. "Well, I would not be able to stand losing him again."

I caught Renie's eye. "Well, we none of us know the future..."

"No. I would not let him leave me. Not for anything. You can be sure of that."

219

She finished her tea and made her excuses. I promised to think upon the plight of the turtles.

Once she had left I looked at Renie.

"Well!" I said.

"Indeed!" she replied.

Neither of us felt the need to say it, but we both knew who was responsible for the letters to Gaskell. She might not have held the pen herself, but the Bishop's lover had certainly arranged for them to be sent. She would not lose him to anything. Even to the Church.

Chapter 36

"Perhaps we are actually getting somewhere with this case," I said to Fort after I had recounted my meeting with Renie and the curious Mrs Faifley.

"I never doubted it for a second," Fort said. "I knew that we would embrace the irresistibleness of things that arrange themselves in mass formations and pass and pass and pass."

I barely even hesitated in my flow. I had become adept at ignoring Fort's linguistic flourishes. "Faifley was definitely responsible for the letter, but I don't think she wrote it herself. Darlington wrote them, I'm sure of it. She stole the ink. So somehow it was arranged between the two of them..."

I thumped my palm on the table. "The explanation is nearly there, I am sure of it."

"As you say," Fort said, searching for something on his desk.

"At least we can be sure there will be no more letters. Not when the culprit is in a coma."

"Ah. Would it change your mind if I showed you something that I received in the first post this morning?"

Fort slid an envelope towards me. I gasped. The paper was instantly recognisable. As was the vivid purple ink.

"It came this morning?" I managed to say. "It came here?"

"Delivered to the office with the alacrity of the British postal system."

"Then it can't be Darlington, unless she can write letters with her mind."

Fort raised an eyebrow.

"I wasn't being serious," I said quickly. I sank down into my chair. Just when I thought I had it all figured out.

And to receive an anonymous letter... I wasn't sure whether to feel angered or strangely flattered.

"It is not surprising that someone might want to target me," I said, "given my recent advancement in circumstances. I suppose I make a fine prospect for blackmail."

Fort grinned. "A lord would be the perfect candidate, would he not? And yet, examine the name on the letter."

I hadn't thought to actually read the front of the envelope.

"Mr Charles Fort. Ah." I blushed while Fort roared out a laugh until his moustache quivered.

"Well," Fort said, wiping his eyes, "shall we find out what indiscretions I have been judged to commit?"

To Mr Charles Fort.

I am writing as your friend. Call off your investigations into these letters or certain events around the coronation of our King will be brought to the attention of the press. I am in possession of photographical evidence. I believe you will understand the significance of this proposal. Cease investigations immediately. I will know if you do not.

I am your friend. Do not make me your enemy.

It was my turn to roar with laughter.

"The Coronation! You truly must have led a blameless life if our anonymous author must resort to such nonsense."

Fort said nothing.

"I mean," I said, the laughter dying on my lips, "could anything be more preposterous?"

Fort said down and curled the end of his moustache around his finger.

"Fort…"

Still silence.

"Fort, you don't mean to say that it's true?"

The American shook his head. "I believe I have underestimated our friend. They appear to have an ability to discover secrets that I had thought long buried. Well, Moreton, what are we going to do about him?"

"Never mind that," I said, "what on earth did you have to do with the coronation of King George?"

"I promised never to say," Fort said with the prim air of an elderly governess.

I gave him my best puppy dog eyes.

"Let us just say that the King was concerned about some… paranormal occurrences that might have prevented his accession to the throne."

"What occurrences were these?"

"I see nothing will comfort you but that I tell you the full story. The soon-to-be-Queen Mary was concerned about the presence of certain spiritual anomalies in Buckingham Palace."

"She was worried about ghosts?"

"Just so."

"And you were employed as what… an exorcist?"

"I think that was what the lady was hoping for. The King himself was rather more reticent. Exorcists are not exactly part of the approved religion, if you get my meaning."

"So what did you do?"

"I tried to appeal to the intellect. I explained one of my theories of these ghostly occurrences. I posited that the things which we call ghosts are merely things that are not in agreement with science. So-called science is, in fact, the least real thing of all. I told him that in point of fact the spiritualists have it all right, but in reverse. There is a ghost-world, but that world is our very own existence. When spirits die they become human beings."

My mouth hung open. "You said this to the King of England? What did he say? Did it convince him to stop worrying about the ghosts?"

"No. Sad to say I believe it went rather over his head."

I snorted back a laugh. "You don't say. What did you do next?"

Fort sighed. "I am not proud of it. But I played the mummer, whispered some esoteric nonsense and declared that the only ghosts were spirits of goodwill and the Royal family had nothing to fear. What can I say, the pay was rather good."

"And the letter-writer seems to know all about this?"

"I cannot think how. But you can imagine how this would be exceedingly embarrassing, not just for my own reputation, but for that of the King of England."

I tapped the desk with my fingernails. "It is a threat, then. We stop investigating the letters or your reputation, and that of the monarchy is tarnished forever."

"Well then, it is lucky that I do not have any reputation to threaten."

"And the King?" I said.

"Probably has other things to worry about. We will continue our investigations, Edward, no matter what the cost."

I stared down at the purple ink. "It's just a pity that this letter rules out our best suspect. Our only suspect, in fact."

"A mere triviality. Although it might be time to call for reinforcements."

Chapter 37

"Threatening one of us? That's just not cricket." O'Connell held the envelope by the edges like it might infect him with some horrible disease.

Fort, I noticed, looked rather pleased with the idea of being called 'one of us' by the burly policeman.

"What does it mean about the King?" O'Connell asked. "It can't be serious, surely?"

Fort and I avoided one another's gaze.

"An exaggeration of course," I said quickly. "Fort is an acquaintance of His Majesty in a... professional capacity."

"Hmmn," O'Connell did not look convinced. "Well, if you don't want to tell me that's your right, I'm sure. How do you think the letter-writer found out about it?"

"It is a puzzle," Fort said, peering at the piece of paper through his gold-rimmed spectacles. "I have told no one about the incident. A few people at the palace knew, but you would imagine they would be used to keeping secrets."

"Someone in government, perhaps?" I suggested.

"There were some minor officials hovering about at the time. Like parasites feeding on a greater creature."

I tried to pretend I wasn't one of the self-same parasites. "Do you remember any of their names."

"Sadly not. And we can hardly ask the King."

O'Connell threw his hands in the air. "Another dead end." He glared at the letter as if it could speak.

"Hold on a second," the policeman said. "Does the writing look different on this one?"

"Does it?" I peered at the letter. It was the familiar purple ink all right, but perhaps there was something... I pulled out my files with the case notes and located the letter to my sister.

"Put it down here, next to the other one," O'Connell instructed. "There! Do you see? The writing doesn't match."

Fort nudged in at my elbow. "I do believe you are correct, Chief Inspector. The slant of the letters is not quite the same. And see here the length of the 'g' below the line... It is a close match, but it seems to me that this new letter is trying to look like it was done by the same hand as the earlier ones. But this letter was written by someone else."

I let out a groan. "You mean we now have two anonymous letter writers?"

"I'm afraid so."

Fort folded his arms. "A quill of letter writers? Or an inkpot perhaps?"

"A crackpot might be more accurate," I grumbled. "Do you know, Chief Inspector, the notion of a second letter writing might just fit with our current theory."

I explained to O'Connell about the stolen ink, and the idea that Eliza Darlington might have written the letters.

"If it was Darlington then that explains the different handwriting. Someone else has taken over where she left off." The Chief Inspector gave me a look bordering on respect. "I don't suppose you know who might have been working with her?"

"Afraid not."

"Well, we can't question Darlington. Not yet at any rate."

"What about O'Hendry?" I said.

O'Connell turned a sharp look onto me. "The man you persuaded me to release, you mean?"

"Ah. Well. He was friendly with Darlington, so…"

"I'll send some Constables around to arrest him again." O'Connell rammed his hat back onto his head and strode out of the door.

"I don't think the Chief Inspector is best pleased," Fort said in a moment of uncharacteristic understatement.

"No, I don't think he is."

Fort put his feet up on his desk. "It is a shame that the government does not pay us on a piecemeal basis. I make our current investigations: one lost manuscript, two dead bodies, two letter writers…"

"Not to mention the cases of the letters themselves: Gaskell's expedition, Mrs Marylebone and her possibly murderous husband, and Colton's drugs."

Fort and I fell silent, each overwhelmed by the task at hand.

"Perhaps we are over complicating the issue," Fort suggested. "Could we be looking at a multi-cellular problem."

"I'm sorry?"

"What about the unification of many parts? What if these separate incidences could be but parts of a greater whole?"

I stared at Fort. "We do have some connections between the cases," I said finally. "But I just cannot see how everything intersects."

"We need some kind of plan. Or a map."

I thought of a certain clothes store owner. "I think I know just where we can find one."

Chapter 38

"Your method is... impressive," Charles Fort said.

Renie Brien let out an audible sigh of relief. "Thank you," she said softly. It never failed to surprise me how different the girl became in the presence of her hero. Perhaps I simply didn't appreciate how someone could be so impressed by the same person I had witnessed trying to see if he could make rocks float.

Fort walked up and down the wall that contained the notes from our investigations into the poison pen letters. He used his forefinger to follow the threads from one piece of paper to another.

I wandered over to my right. Since I had last visited Renie had added another section to her spiderweb of facts.

"What's this over here?" I asked.

"That's the information from the Cutler murder."

"But that shouldn't be part of the poison pen case, surely?"

"Do you think so?" Renie came over and stood next to me. "Look at the threads. There are plenty of connections to suggest that this is all one case."

"All one case..." I realised then that I had already been thinking of the poison pens, the missing manuscript and Cutler's death as the same case. I just needed someone to remind me.

"See this section, for example." Renie pointed to a confluence of red threads. "Here we have Virginia Woolf. She is connected to the missing manuscript of course, because she knew O'Hendry. She is publisher, like Cutler, although there is nothing to suggest she was involved in his death. But she is also the recipient of at least one anonymous letter. And Colton had one of her books in his pocket when he died. She connects everything."

"But she is not our murderer," I said, "I am certain of that."

"Perhaps she is the catalyst," Fort said. "She is part of any of these schemes, but her very existence is critical to all of them."

I sighed. "I suppose I should go back to Bloomsbury."

Fort nodded. "This time I am coming with you."

This time I decided to wait until Leonard Woolf had gone for his evening constitutional before approaching the house. I had a feeling that the man might not let me in.

"Mr Moreton," Mrs Woolf managed a smile when she opened the door, but it was rather strained. "And you have brought Mr Fort. Please come in."

Charles Fort headed immediately to his standard position in these situations: he went to look at her bookshelves.

"I'm sorry to bother you once again Mrs Woolf, but I wondered if you could share your story of the Dreadnought hoax with my colleague here."

"Again? You must be tired of hearing the story of our silly little prank. I am growing tired of telling it."

"Mrs Woolf, we have this morning received an anonymous letter threatening my colleague here and no less a personage than the King himself. I cannot help but feel that you are keeping something back. Anything at all that you can tell us will be helpful."

The author hugged her arms across her chest. "I was asked by a good friend not to speak of it."

"Mrs Woolf, your loyalty is to your credit. But I am looking for a cold-blooded murderer. I am not interested in state secrets or conspiracies. I just want to find a killer."

"You had better sit down." Fort reluctantly left the bookshelves and we both took seating positions on a worn-looking chesterfield.

"I told you last time that the prank had been initiated to serve as a distraction. That is true. We were asked to perform our little ruse so that a team of investigators might gain access to the ship. There was a fear that someone on board was deliberately targeting the young men."

"Targeting them?"

"Turning them into addicts."

A chill pricked its way up my spine. "Let me guess. Cocaine."

"There have always been drug-takers in the military, of course," Mrs Woolf explained. "It would be foolish to pretend otherwise. We all have our little peccadillos. Have you ever tried chloral? I find it soothes the mind when nothing else will."

"So it wasn't secret documents they sent you for. It was cocaine that you were looking for on the Dreadnought?" I asked, bringing the conversation back to the subject at hand.

"Yes, or rather, the supplier of it. We were to provide a distraction while the boat was searched." Her face lit up. "We certainly did that. It was rather fun. In spite of everything I must thank you for reminding me of it."

"Did they find the person who supplied the cocaine?"

"No. I think they may have apprehended a few of the young men that were addicts, but the man at the top evaded them."

I nodded at Fort. Finally, we had reached the truth of it. And it couldn't be a coincidence that cocaine was involved.

"That reminds me," I said, reaching into my pocket. "I brought you this." I handed her the copy of Kew Gardens that had been found on Colton's corpse.

"This was the one recovered from the dead man?" Woolf said as she took it gently from my outstretched hand.

"Yes. I know it is a little… unseemly. But I didn't want it to just be put in the bin."

"Thank you." She looked at it curiously. "You have read it, of course?"

In actual fact I hadn't bothered. But I hardly wanted to disappoint the lady.

"Of course," I replied.

Woolf smiled. "What did you think of the ending?"

"Oh, marvellous. Marvellous."

"Is that right?" She turned the book around and opened it at the back. Someone had glued together the last dozen or so pages.

"Ah…"

"Shall we see what is inside?" Mrs Woolf reached for a letter opened and poked a small hole into the sealed pages. She turned the book upside down and a thin trickle of powder came out.

"You do not have to be a great mind to guess what this is," Virginia Woolf said with a grin.

Chapter 39

We returned to the office rejuvenated by our conversation with Virginia Woolf. Finally, we had tangible evidence. Colton was still supplying cocaine and he had been carrying it when he was killed. Despite Fort's love for theory, I couldn't help but feel pleased with our discovery of material evidence. The Chief Inspector would be pleased.

My euphoria lasted right up until the moment that I opened the office door and found Maurice Hankey waiting for me.

"Good day, Fort. Moreton."

My heart sank. There was no means of escape now. For one desperate moment I thought of flinging myself out of the window.

"I haven't seen you all week, Mr Moreton. You haven't been avoiding me, have you?"

"Of course not, sir."

Fort, unaware of the undercurrent of tension in the room, gave our superior a nod of recognition then sat down in at his desk, immediately immersing himself in a book.

"We have to talk about what happens to your cases."

I glanced at Fort but he didn't look up.

"Could we do this later, sir? It's just we have found some rather compelling evidence –"

"There is no later! I have been wanting to discuss your elevation for days. As I am sure you are aware, you are now out of time."

"Edward," Fort had finally realised that something serious was going on, "what does Mr Hankey mean by your 'elevation'?"

I ran a hand through my hair. I hadn't wanted him to find out like this, but I was out of time.

"You know that I have inherited the Dukedom."

"I could hardly have avoided the fact."

"Well, it comes with estates, land, the usual things. But it also comes with a rather important Peerage."

"I'm sorry, you remember that I am not from this country. What are you trying to say?"

"The Duke of Bentham has a seat in the House of Lords," Hankey said with an irritated tone. "A position that has been held for generations. And if one is a member of the Lords…"

"Then I cannot also work for the Civil Service," I concluded for him. "I'm sorry, Fort. When I inherited the title it was only a matter of time before they would insist I take my position in the upper house. I don't have a choice."

"And when do you need to take up this position?"

"Monday," Hankey said curtly.

For once, Fort was speechless and I couldn't even enjoy the moment, so wretched was the expression on the man's face.

"We just need a little more time, sir," I said. "We are close to discovering both the letter writer and the murderer of two men. If you could just give me a little longer."

I looked around the room, a drowning man desperate for a life raft, but there was nothing there.

"There is no more time. Mr Fort may complete the case, then his position with the service will be re-evaluated. As for yourself, I think you will have quite enough to be getting on with."

"But, sir –"

"Clear your desk, Moreton. Do it now."

Hankey stalked out of the room. My partner and I stared at one another. Then, very slowly, Fort picked up his book and left the office. The last thing I saw was the light glinting off Charles Fort's spectacles as he closed the door.

Outside the sun shone and the people of London smiled at one another in the unseasonable warmth. Through the happiness of the crowd I stalked like the ghost at the feast. Gloom and melancholia surrounded me, a palpable aura.

I had been walking rather aimlessly since my run-in with Hankey and had ended up in Hyde Park. I threw a crust of bread to the ducks and watched them squabble with one another to pluck the pieces from the water.

"Lovely day, isn't it?"

Victoria MacMillan looked resplendent in the crisp morning sunlight. Her eyes twinkled with good humour as she sat down next to me on the bench.

"I suppose you haven't heard. I've been fired."

"Oh, I heard all right. It's quite the topic of conversation in the typing pool."

"Well, you needn't look so pleased about it."

She laughed. "Come now, Edward, this moping around really does not suit you. Do you really think that I would be happy about you losing your job? I know how much you loved it."

"Did I love it?" I gazed out at the ducks who were wiggling their way back to the centre of the pond. "I suppose I did, in a way. It's Fort I feel bad about, mostly. I can't help feeling that I let him down."

"Charles Fort is a grown man, Edward," Victoria said. "You are not responsible for him."

"I don't want to be a Peer of the Realm. I will look utterly ridiculous in ermine."

"Then do something else."

I bit my lip. "I don't see how it's possible. I cannot be a Duke and continue in my job. Hankey has made it perfectly clear. It is against the rules."

Victoria sat on the wall next to the pond and swung her legs back and forth.

"I'm not here to tell you what to do, Edward. That's not my place."

"But Vic –"

She held up her hand. "I won't do it. It is your life to lead. But perhaps I could give you a little advice."

She reached forward and grabbed my chin, as a mother might do to a recalcitrant child.

"For God's sake chose *something!*" She laughed as I nearly fell backward from the force of her words.

"And whatever I chose," I said as she started to walk away. "Will you still be there?"

The only answer was a languid wave of her hand as she disappeared around a bend in the path.

Chapter 40

I slunk back into my office. After all, where else was I supposed to go? To my surprise, Fort was back at his desk as if nothing had happened.

"Hello Edward."

"Fort. Um, I'm sorry about before."

The American waved a hand dismissively. "Was I put out that you hadn't confided in me? Yes. But I am nothing if not a pragmatist. If we are to only have a little more time together, then surely we should spend it in solving this final case."

I was touched and my voice was a little unsteady as I replied. "Just as you say, Fort."

"To that end, I have consulted our notes once more. Do you remember your fugitive waiter?"

"The one that absconded from Brown's after eavesdropping on Renie and me?"

"The very same. You left his address on your desk. As you never had the chance to follow it up, I did it for you."

Fort sat back in his chair looking rather pleased with himself. "The address was a rather squalid flat near the docks. I managed to corner the waiter and by the administration of a small sum of money I have elicited some information. I hope that I will be reimbursed."

"If it is the last thing I do you will get your money back."

We both paused at the idea that it might be just that.

"Anyway," Fort said, his cheeks a little pink, "the man was sorely in need of income. Not only had he abandoned his job at the hotel, his roommate had recently been murdered.

I stared at Fort. "The man was Colton's roommate?"

"Exactly."

"Well, go on, what did he tell you?"

Charles Fort rested his thumbs in his waistcoat. "He told a diverting little tale. Apparently, he and Colton were old Navy chums. Mickey Colton had got himself involved in a scheme, some sort of petty blackmail. Colton asked this waiter to keep his nose to the ground, look out for anyone who might become a potential client."

"A client?"

"People tell each other secrets over a cup of tea, that's what the waiter said. They never think about who might be listening in. If, for example, someone had a problem with a person, say an old lady who wouldn't cough up on an inheritance, then our waiter would suggest someone who could help them."

"Someone who might write them a letter?"

"Just so."

I could almost feel the shape of the solution, even though I couldn't quite articulate it yet. I leaned forward in concentration.

"Our waiter overhears someone complaining about something. He passes them over to Colton. Colton arranges for the blackmail letters to be sent, for a large fee I would imagine."

"Exactly."

"And who wrote the letters?"

"The waiter doesn't know. He said he knew it wasn't Colton, but other than that... he was kept deliberately out of it."

"The ink suggests that it was Darlington that wrote the letters. Only… only Darlington is unconscious and Colton is dead. Which means that someone else sent us the most recent letter addressed to you."

"Telephone for Moreton!" A voice shouted down the corridor. I hurried over to the machine and pressed the receiver to my ear.

"It's Renie. I can't talk for long. I tracked down the nephew of Mrs Marylebone."

"The respectable GP?"

"That's the one. Turns out he likes to spend his Saturdays at the track."

"Horses?"

"Exactly. Turns out he's in a spot of bother with someone called Ernie the Hat. You English have such colourful names."

"Thanks Renie."

"Your welcome. And you owe me threepence for the call." The line went dead.

I hurried back to the office and told Fort the news.

"Sounds like the nephew was one of Colton's 'clients'," I said. "Although it'll be the devil to prove."

Fort shrugged. "There was one other thing. The waiter had been given a package by Colton. He called it his 'security'."

Like a magician at a variety show, Fort reached under his desk and brought out a package wrapped in brown paper.

I ripped the paper off, already all too aware of what I would find. A stack of paper with the title 'Intransigent Delphinium' written across the front.

"But, Fort, that means… Oh hell, I have made rather a bloody mess of it all."

"You have brought me here to arrest Mr O'Hendry," Chief Inspector O'Connell said as we walked towards the author's home.

"That's right."

"The man that I arrested and then released on your suggestion."

"Correct."

To O'Connell's credit, he opted for sullen silence rather than a punch to the jaw.

Fort pounded on the door. "Open up, it's the law!" He caught sight of the Chief Constable's face.

"Sorry, got a little over excited."

It seemed to do the job, as the door was presently opened by a pipe smoking O'Hendry.

He looked from Fort to the Chief Inspector, until his eyes settled on me.

"I wondered how long you would be. The poets tell us that Justice is blind. They never mentioned how bloody slow she is. Would you rather we do it here or at the police station. I can offer you a brandy?"

"Down at the station," O'Connell said. "But you'll be glad to know we have arranged your transportation."

In truth, the ride in the Black Maria was almost comfortable. I had to remind myself that I was sat in the company of a murderer.

When we got into the interview room O'Hendry couldn't wait

to confess.

"I've been waiting for you to work it out for days. Days! I almost felt like giving you clues."

"You wanted to be caught?" The Chief Inspector sounded incredulous.

"Well… not exactly. But you found the book, didn't you? My fingerprints must be all over it."

I avoided O'Connell's eyes. The book had been fingerprinted of course, but the policeman had told us earlier he was still waiting for the results.

"It was a petty revenge, but a satisfying one."

"The murder of Colton?"

"No, the desecration of the stupid woman's book. You have no idea how much I enjoyed gluing the pages together so no other poor fool would have to read it.

"Let's get back to the blackmail," O'Connell said firmly. "It was a nice little enterprise you built for yourself. You had Darlington write the letters for you. Mickey Colton was there to connect you with your… clients."

O'Hendry nodded. "Clever, don't you think? That was we never had to meet any of them face to face. It was foolproof."

"Until it wasn't. What went wrong?"

"Intransigent Delphinium."

O'Connell blinked. "What?"

"It's the name of his novel," I explained. "The one that went missing."

"I truly did think someone had stolen it. And I had maybe been taking a little too much of the powder, so that my first thought was to involve you lot."

"You invited the police to your house even though you were involved in drug running and blackmail."

"As I said, I had been sampling my own wears a little too keenly. Anyway, when I thought about it a bit more I thought that maybe Darlington had taken it."

"Why would she do that?"

For the first time O'Hendry looked ashamed. "She… assisted in some of it. Just minor details you understand. The body of the work was mine."

"You had Darlington write your novel for you?" Charles Fort said, appalled.

"It wasn't like that! I was on a deadline, Cutler wanted the manuscript finished… she just helped out a little that's all."

This seemed to be what O'Hendry was most ashamed of. Getting someone else to write his book.

"But Darlington didn't steal the manuscript. Colton gave it to his roommate."

"Is that where it ended up. I thought she'd left it with the publisher. We had a row. She wanted out of the blackmail game. She said that if I didn't stop with the letters she would tell St John Cutler exactly who had written the book."

"So you did kill Cutler?"

O'Hendry laughed. "I did enjoy all that time you spent fighting for my innocence, Mr Moreton. Of course I killed him. Only not because of a lost manuscript. That would be ridiculous."

"Why then?"

"Because he was going to tell them all! It was the damned

parodies. She just couldn't resist putting them in. Cutler recognised the style from an article she wrote about Simmonds. He called me up, told me he was going to pull the book. He said that if I didn't give back the advance he'd tell Mr Moreton here all about it."

"It was the money, then?"

"I needed it."

"For drugs?"

O'Hendry simply shrugged.

"And why did you attack Darlington?"

"Why did she have to do it?"

"Do what?"

"Those bloody parodies. I never even knew they were there until Cutler read Delphinium. She just had to put that little bit of cleverness in. Show she was smarter than the rest of us. Well, she didn't look so smart with her brains bashed in."

O'Hendry smiled a sickly smile.

"She's going to be all right," I said, gripping my coat to stop myself from punching the man in the face. "The doctors say she'll make a full recovery."

"Another kick in the teeth for modern art," O'Hendry muttered.

O'Connell stood up. "My Sargeant here will charge you for Cutler's death and the attack on Eliza Darlington. Not to mention the little matter of the murder of Mickey Colton.

"Hang on a minute. Look, I'll admit I bashed Cutler over the head. I didn't think the old man would die. It was heat of the moment, all right? And Darlington… well… she shouldn't have messed around with the manuscript. It was my reputation on

244

the line, not hers. Anyway, I didn't plan for any of it. Yes, I made some mistakes, but I certainly didn't stab Colton."

"That's for the jury to decide."

Chapter 41

"They are all mad, the whole lot of them," I said to Fort as we made our way back from the police station.

"They are authors!" Fort exclaimed. "Just what do you expect?"

"Do you believe he killed Colton?"

"The evidence seems to suggest he did…"

"Do you mind if we make a quick stop before we go back to the office?"

"Not at all."

I paid for the cab to Richmond Park and left Fort waiting while I went inside. I could have waited until later, but I wanted to speak to her while the poison pen case was fresh in my mind.

"Your sister is in the parlour," my mother said when I walked into the hall.

I took a deep breath. "It's not Liz that I've come to see. Can we go upstairs?"

My legs felt heavy as I climbed up the stairs to my mother's room. It smelt like my mother always did, of lilies and regret.

"It is good to see you, Edward," my mother said as she sat down on the window seat.

Her eyelids were heavy. I wondered just how much sedative she had been given. Was she truly grieving my father? I suppose that she had loved him to some extent, as impossible as the thought might be.

"Mother." I kissed the hand that she proffered to me.

"I have been sending cards to all your father's friends. A good turnout for the funeral, didn't you think?"

"Very good," I said. "And how are you doing, mother?"

"I endure, my darling. Your sister is very good to me."

The room was already making me feel claustrophobic. There were too many flowers. They made me think of the graveside.

"I need to talk to you about something."

My mother smiled. "You want to make arrangements to take over the estates. Well, I won't say you haven't taken your time about it…"

Courage, I told myself. You need to survive this room long enough to get some answers.

"I wanted to ask you about the letters."

She indicated her desk. "I have written a dozen already this morning."

"It is not those letters I have come to talk about."

Was that a flicker of recognition on her face?

"What do you mean?"

"Did you know that Liz has been receiving some anonymous letters?"

Once again, my mother's reply was just a fraction too slow, a little too considered.

"No. She has not mentioned any letters."

"Poison pen letters, they are called."

My mother's hand shook a little as she reached up to replace a loose curl of silver-blond hair. "Are they? I wouldn't know about such things. I suppose the criminal element is much more in your line of work."

247

I took a deep breath. "When did you find out about the cocaine?"

This time the recognition on my mother's face was unmistakable.

"Cocaine?"

"Come on now, mother. I know that you know. Liz has been using cocaine. Ever since the war."

Now the woman finally turned to face me. Her cheeks were powdered and her lips red, her hair just as perfectly arranged as ever. But there were dark circles around her eyes, and I was sure there were new lines on her forehead. Worry lines.

"Do we have to do this now?"

"I'm afraid so."

"Your father is dead, you callous child."

A took in a ragged breath. "I know. But you must talk to me about Liz. For her sake."

My mother's shoulders sagged. "You were always one of those children who could never let anything go. Why, why, why, that's all you asked when you were a child. I had thought that your father had taught you all you needed to know about asking too many questions."

"Even the cane couldn't stop me doing that," I said softly. "Tell me about Liz."

"I'm not sure when it started. I first noticed it at the party we had for Armistice. There was something... wild about her eyes. I tried to put it down to youthful excitement. She was terribly bored during the war, you see. It was a dreadful time for our sort of people, with all the young men away. We could never get up a decent dance or a dinner table."

I stayed silent, which, under the circumstances, felt rather heroic.

"She had a little box. I thought it was snuff or something. But then I realised it was this powder. Well… I didn't think much of it. Sherry or cocaine, it's much the same. But there was a problem."

"Mickey Colton?"

A grim nod. "That was the problem with the drug. It forced one into the basest sort of company. I tried talking to her. Well, you know your sister, I might as well have spoken to a stone. She was determined to keep up her disgusting assignations with the man just to get her powders."

"Then the war ended. Colton disappeared off somewhere and I thought that was an end to it."

"Until he came back."

"It was going so well!" My mother wailed. "Henry Fashton! He may be new money but at least he's got a title of sorts. I thought I would finally get her married off. Then Colton turns up again and puts everything I have worked for at risk."

"And the letters?"

She said nothing, just stared at me.

"You didn't write them yourself. I know that. The same person that wrote to Liz wrote to Bishop Gaskell and Mrs Marylebone."

"Dreadful common names."

I ignored the blood rising in my brain. "So how was it done?"

"I arranged for the letters to be written," she said softly. "A daughter of a friend of mine suggested someone who could help with the problem. A very stupid man, but someone who was useful.

"O'Hendry?"

"Was that his name? He thought himself a poet. It was easily arranged. The letters were artfully written, I will give the fellow that."

How did we come to this? I thought, and I felt a pang of pity for the woman, in spite of it all.

"Why did you do it, mother?"

When her voice finally answered it was old and cracked. "I did it to save her. I did it to save my daughter."

I almost laughed out loud. "But the lies... All that hurt and deception. Was that really the best way you could think of?"

"What else could I do? She would never listen to me. Neither of you have ever listened to your mother. I have never expected gratitude for what I have done for you both. But I did it anyway. Because that is what mother's do."

The anger flared up once more. "Gratitude? For what? Perhaps if you had stood up to father..."

"Enough!"

"Mother..."

"I want you to leave. Right now. And don't bother coming back until you have learned to show some respect."

I walked out of the room, slamming the door behind me. I turned away from my mother's room and walked straight into Liz.

"Did you know that she was responsible for the letters?"

Liz dabbed at her eyes with a silk handkerchief. We had made our way to the drawing room in silence, hand in hand, just as we had as children.

"No. At least, not for certain."

"But you wondered?"

"Not until a few days ago. I was... upset after Mickey's death. She told me that I had to get over it for the sake of my engagement. It was a little too like the words in the letter to be a coincidence."

I snorted. "I'm just glad she has an alibi for his death. He was killed during father's funeral, you know."

Liz winced. "I did like him. It wasn't just about the drugs. Oh, Edward, is this all my fault?"

I put my hand on hers. "You are not responsible for what our mother did. I know you, Liz. You are not a bad person."

"I don't know what I am." She shivered and I grabbed a shawl to wrap around her shoulders. It was strange and unpleasant to see my sister so vulnerable. She had always been the strong one.

"I must get back to Fort," I said. "I need to tell him about mother."

"Will she be in trouble?"

"Nothing money can't buy her out of." I saw Liz's face. "Sorry. No, I shouldn't think the Chief Inspector will want to prosecute her for anything."

"And what will you do now, Edward?"

"Me? I shall go back to work." For as long as I can, I added in my head.

"Why is this job so important to you. I wouldn't say you were a laughing stock —"

"You have before."

"Perhaps. But I was being unkind. You must admit however that it is an odd choice of profession."

"For a… a Duke?" I could still hardly bring myself to say the word.

"Millions would kill for the privilege of your position. You can have anything you want."

That statement was so patently false, I couldn't help but burst out laughing. Liz looked at me for a few seconds then she started to giggle.

"I'm sorry, Edward," she said in between gasps of laughter. "I'm being an idiot."

"And I'm sorry I've been such a wretched brother," I said once the hysterics had subsided. "I'll be better from now on."

"No you won't," Liz said with another laugh. "But that's all right. I'm a pretty wretched sister."

We fell back into silence, but it was a friendlier silence now.

"I have to ask, Liz. The cocaine. Are you really over it?"

"I am trying to be."

I nodded. That would have to do.

"And I'm sorry I didn't tell you about it sooner. You're not really angry with me, are you Edward?"

I sighed. "Of course not. I just wish you'd trust me a little more."

"That's just what Mickey said. To trust him. Then he drove away in that fancy car and never looked back."

"Fancy car?" The room seemed very still all of a sudden. "He didn't seem like he had enough spare cash to run a motorcar."

"I don't think it was his. Somebody picked him up. I saw them right out of the window." Liz sniffed. "It wasn't as pretty as your Rolls. But it went like the clappers."

A sinking feeling was growing in the pit of my stomach. "A fast car, did you say? You didn't happen to see who was driving?"

Chapter 42

"Take us to Long Acre as fast as you can!"

My shout to the driver woke Fort from slumber in the back of the cab.

"What in the name of the damned is going on?" Fort asked as the wheels thumped over the cobbles.

"O'Hendry was telling the truth. He didn't kill Colton. He couldn't have done anyway, he was in the cells at the time accused of Cutler's murder."

"Then who...?"

"A man with a fast car!"

"In Long Acre?"

"The Austin showroom is there. They are releasing a new line today, there's no way the Sailor will be anywhere else."

"You think that this Sailor character killed Colton?"

"Liz saw him drive away in his Austin. It's a one of a kind."

"But why?"

"That's what we're going to find out!"

Fort clung on to the door as the cab rattled around a sharp bend. Before he could say anything else we screeched to a halt outside the Austin showroom.

"We should have picked up O'Connell on the way."

"I didn't think of that," I said, cursing myself. I had been too excited by my discovery to wait for reinforcements.

"I'll go on in," I said after a moment's thought. "He knows me and he doesn't think I'm a threat. You go and get the cab to take you to the police station. It's only ten minutes away."

"Are you sure?"

"Of course. I'll get him by himself somehow. He's an old man, I can take care of myself."

Fort nodded and shouted some instructions to the driver and they zoomed away again, horn blaring.

I walked into the Austin showroom. It had been spruced up for the launch of the 1661 cc Twelve. I walked past a line of the cars, all gleaming and new. The place was busy. I weaved in and out of men in smart coats and hats, looking for one gentleman in particular.

I spotted an engineer I vaguely recognised from the track.

"All right Frank, you seen the Sailor about at all?"

"He's in the back looking at the luxury models. This stuffs all a bit prosaic for the likes of him."

I nodded and manoeuvred my way to the rear of the showroom. The luxury cars were through an archway into a land of gleaming chrome and aluminium.

Lady luck was in my favour. The Sailor was on his own standing next to an old four-cylinder model in racing colours.

"Moreton! Good to see you, old boy."

I shook his hand being careful not to betray the agitation I felt in my face. I hoped that Fort was on his way.

"You're thinking of buying something?" I asked idly.

"I'm always in the market, of course. Especially something with racing pedigree."

He was about to leave. I couldn't let that happen. I placed my hand on his arm.

"There was something else I wanted to ask you about concerning the death of Mickey Colton."

The movement came so quickly that I wasn't expecting it. I didn't even have a chance to raise my hands in self defence as the Sailor sprung at me.

I tried to shout out for help but the wind was knocked out of me as Windmore wrestled me to the floor. The man's hands closed upon my neck. I tried again to scream but could only manage a strangled gurgle.

Dark spots appeared before my eyes and my last thought was that the papers would announce my death as that of the bloody Duke of bloody Bentham.

Suddenly Windmore careened backward, shrieking and clutching at his back. He whirled around and I saw a pair of scissors protruding from a wound in his back. Behind him was a rather startled looking Charles Fort.

"Whoever said the pen was mightier than the sword overlooked a still mightier weapon – the scissors," Fort said as he wiped the sweat from his brow.

Chief Inspector O'Connell appeared beside the Sailor and put a pair of handcuffs on him.

"Just a flesh wound," the policeman announced after examining our captive's back.

"What sort of cowardly blackguard stabs a man in the back," Windmore complained.

"A far more sensible one than attacks from the front," Fort said. He was holding his spectacles and carefully adjusting one of the legs until they were perfectly symmetrical once more.

I leaned back on the cool metal of the bonnet of the grand prix car. My hands were shaking so much I stuck them in my pockets so the others couldn't see.

"Why did you kill Colton?" I asked.

Windmore grimaced. "The man was a bloody liability. I should have known better than to trust him with the blackmail business. I had started him off through one of my suppliers. Cocaine, you understand."

"Was this on the Dreadnought?"

"Not as foolish as you look, are you Moreton. Well, Colton was fine as a supplier of my little powders, but anything that required even a little intelligence…"

"You killed him because he was too much of a risk to stay your little scheme?"

"He was never meant to know who I was. I had a string of men in between myself and Colton. But somehow he worked out who was in charge. I guess he might have spotted me on at Browns, but I can't know for sure. Anyway, as soon as he put two and two together he decided to try his own little spot of blackmail. Can you imagine the nerve of it, threatening me with exposure!"

Another policeman had turned up, along with a doctor who settled down to the unenviable task of removing the scissors from Windmore's back.

"I think we'll leave it to you, Chief Inspector," I said, turning my back on the grisly scene.

"You're a second-rate driver, you know that!" Windmore yelled as Fort and I hurried out of the door.

"I never liked sore losers," Fort muttered as we made our way back to the cab.

I felt the excitement of the day drain from my body, leaving me feeling utterly hallowed out and spent.

"Hankey will be waiting for me at the office," I said.

The American nodded. "He will be, yes."

"Fort... I don't know what to do."

Charles Fort blinked at me through his spectacles. "A wise man once wrote: 'to thine own self be true'."

I groaned. "Let me guess, it's from your Book of the Damned. Or the new one you just submitted, what's it called again?

Fort coughed. "Actually, it's from Hamlet. My point being: who the devil do you want to be anyway? Time to make your choice."

Epilogue

"Can't this thing go any faster?"

I risked a quick glance to my right. Victoria somehow managed to look beautiful in an overall and goggles. I could just see her red lipstick as she opened her mouth to shriek while we went around the bend.

"You're not scared?" I said as I opened up the throttle.

"Me?" She laughed, "Not on your life!"

I spun the wheel, pushing the Rolls deeper into the next corner. The wheels screamed as the car shimmied sideways.

"Back at work tomorrow?" Victoria shouted as I adjusted my goggles with one hand and steered with the other.

"Of course. The extraordinary phenomena of the criminal classes wait for no man."

"I'm sure I don't understand half of what you say, but I'm glad that you'll be staying for a while."

"Can't let Fort do it all on his own, can I? He's already asked if I'll re-order his notes over the summer. He's got a new book to write. Something about literary genius and wild talents. He'll have me proof reading the blasted thing. And Hankey's told me I better do some training in hand to hand combat. Says it embarrassing that the old American keeps saving my skin."

"Was that before or after you abdicated?"

My laugh was lost in the growl of the engine. "Abdication is for Kings!"

"Gave up the Lords then," Victoria shouted. "Respectfully declined a position in the House. I would have loved to have seen Hankey's face!"

"Not sure he'll put up with me for much longer, member of the Lords or not. But for the moment…" I paused to shift gears. "For the moment I can stay."

"And how does that feel?"

We raced along the straight to the finish line, a silver blur on the very edge of control.

"It feels like freedom!"

With apologies to Virginia Woolf...

I have taken one or two liberties with the Bloomsbury set, but I like to believe that the spirit of those times has been conveyed accurately. The Dreadnought hoax did genuinely happen, and it caused a bit of a stir for the Royal Navy at the time. Was there any more to it than a silly prank? I have always wondered...

Any aspersions cast on members of the literary establishment, or indeed the Royal family are entirely fictional.

The irrepressible Renie Brien will be featuring in her own series of novels coming soon, and look out for more Charles Fort Historical Mysteries coming in 2020.